A Hopeful Bride
Crest Stone Mail-Order Brides, Book 1
by Cat Cahill

D1526944

Copyright

---

1. http://www.catcahill.com/

Chapter One

CREST STONE, COLORADO Territory — May 1876

He needed a wife.

Roman Carlisle dug a spoon into the barely edible gruel. The dancing lamplight created shadows that hid the food in his bowl, which was likely a good thing. The horses in his livery stable had a better supper than this one.

"It turned out decent this time," Jeremiah Wiley said with far more enthusiasm than Roman could pretend to muster.

Roman shoved another spoonful of the bland mush into his mouth. It crunched as he chewed, and he made a face into the shadows away from Jeremiah. It was either eat this or spend precious coins purchasing a meal. And when that money could be better spent on hay or a new horse or any number of other items, Roman would opt to stomach Jeremiah's sad attempts at cooking.

The money he saved could also pay for an advertisement for a wife and the funds she needed to travel here.

Roman shoved the thought away and forced himself to scoop out the remainder of the gruel before telling Jeremiah he was going to check on the horses one last time before they turned in. They didn't have many—not yet—but he'd only opened the livery a couple of weeks ago. The spring chill crept in around the newly built stable as he stopped by each stall. Most of the horses were boarded, but Roman owned three himself. He rented two of those out to anyone who needed a mount and had the funds to pay for one.

He paused by the makeshift desk near the front of the stable, where he sat and pulled the letter from his pocket again. It had arrived from Roman's mother two days ago, and while it contained her usual news about his brothers and their wives and children, this one had stirred something inside Roman.

He wanted what his brothers had. A wife. And children. And a house.

It had been on his mind so much the last couple of days that he'd gone and measured the portion of his land behind the livery's corral, curious how many rooms he could fit into a house back there. And then earlier today, he'd found himself watching three of the only children in the new little town running around the partially built church. And then later in the afternoon . . .

Roman's face went warm as he remembered it. He'd stopped by the newly finished land office building and spoken with Jake Gilbert. Not about purchasing land or any number of things he might speak about to Gilbert. Instead, he asked him if it was true his wife was going to start up a mail-order bride advertising business.

He had to give Gilbert credit. The man Roman had only known for a couple of months hadn't laughed at him or asked why he couldn't find a girl on his own. In fact, Gilbert had grinned, slapped him on the back, and told him to stop by the room he shared with his wife at the Crest Stone Hotel tomorrow.

Now tomorrow was but a few hours away, and Roman didn't have the remotest idea of what to expect. But if he didn't turn yellow, he'd be on his way to having everything he wanted.

He'd no longer be a worthless cowboy, drifting and spending money as soon as he got it. He'd be a respectable businessman, with a wife and family. Every bit as good as his brothers.

"TELL ME A LITTLE ABOUT yourself, Mr. Carlisle." Mrs. Gilbert's voice was soft and kind, and she gave him a reassuring nod as he settled himself into the chair beside a small desk.

Jake Gilbert had busied himself with some reading across the room, but Roman still felt on display. This entire situation was awkward, to say the least.

Mrs. Gilbert glanced at her husband, before turning her dark eyes back to Roman. "You aren't the first man who's asked to place an advertisement, despite the fact that Mrs. Young and I haven't fully set up our business yet."

"Mrs. Young?" He was new to the area, but Roman had met most of the men in Crest Stone. He didn't recall a Young.

"She's a dear friend of mine in Cañon City. Her husband is the county sheriff. We both collect advertisements, and then she will have them printed at the newspaper office there."

"Ah, I see." Roman shifted in his chair, wondering if it were too late to run for the door. Surely he could find some worthwhile woman if he spent some time in Cañon City.

Except that would mean leaving his livery for who knew how long, and that would be impossible if he wanted the business to survive. Jeremiah couldn't run the place on his own. He either placed his advertisement with Mrs. Gilbert's service and hoped for the best, or he waited around for a year or two in the hopes a single, respectable lady might arrive in Crest Stone. Of course, then he'd be competing with every other man in town.

"Considering this town is seeing more men every day," Mrs. Gilbert said, "and most of the only eligible ladies around work in this hotel and aren't allowed to be courted—"

"Didn't much stop me," Gilbert said from his seat in the corner.

His wife's olive skin blushed a dark red. "Jake, you aren't helping."

He shot her a grin, and Roman was torn between wanting to be elsewhere and wishing for something exactly like these two had. He'd heard all about the Gilbert Girls working at the hotel's restaurant—and had even been served by a few the handful of times he'd dined at the hotel's lunch counter. They were friendly young women from places far more civilized than the rugged Colorado mountains, and whose livelihoods depended upon keeping spotless reputations.

Of course, he'd also heard that Jake Gilbert was somehow related to the family who owned the hotel and several others like it. Why a man of such means lived in a small room with his wife and worked at the land office in remote Crest Stone was a mystery. Roman imagined there was an interesting story behind Gilbert's situation.

"Once the land office is more established, I'll be able to set up business there. I imagine the men in town seeking wives will find it much more conducive to their privacy." Mrs. Gilbert's gaze slid to her husband, who smiled behind his book. "Now where were we?"

"You asked me about myself." Roman shifted again. "I'm afraid there isn't much to say. I run the livery, as you know. I come from a large family in Kansas City."

"What made you come here?" Mrs. Gilbert asked as she wrote with a pencil on a piece of paper in front of her.

It was an easy question, and a hard one at the same time. He settled for saying, "I like horses and thought I wanted to work a ranch."

"You were a cowboy?"

Roman decided that not much got past Mrs. Gilbert. He nodded, and added quickly, "But I realized that wasn't the life for me. I prefer something more settled. Something I can make my own."

She nodded approvingly, and he felt as if he'd passed some sort of test in school.

Mrs. Gilbert tapped her pencil on the desk. "Our service is different because Mrs. Young and I want to place advertisements only for men of good quality and high moral standards. You see, we want to assure the women who answer these ads that the men placing them are good, honest men who are able to provide for them. It's asking a lot, you know, to give up your entire life, travel to a place you've never been, and take a chance on someone you've never met."

Roman consciously tried not to shift in his chair. He had the strangest feeling, as if he were sitting at his mother's table, about to hear a lecture on his poor choices and wayward path in life.

Except, he wasn't that man anymore. He hoped Mrs. Gilbert could see that.

"Normally, I'd be skeptical of a cowhand, but you've started a good business here. My husband speaks highly of you, and you seem to be of a good nature."

Roman let out a shaky breath, hoping Mrs. Gilbert didn't see how nervous she'd made him.

She straightened her pencil. "Now, tell me what sort of lady you'd like to meet."

He hadn't thought much on that, beyond vague imaginings of someone soft and pretty with an easy smile and—of course—the ability to make something more edible than Jeremiah's gruel. He rambled on, letting Mrs. Gilbert fill in the gaps for him.

"I'll send this up to Mrs. Young on the next train," Mrs. Gilbert said as she stood. "We're planning to get the advertisements printed and mailed to various cities back East by next week, which means you ought to be receiving some correspondence soon."

Roman paid for the advertisement and thanked Mrs. Gilbert. He left the hotel with her husband, who thankfully talked of everything but what had just happened.

By the time he reached the livery, Roman was smiling at nothing at all. What sort of lady might write to him? What would he do if he received multiple letters? The thought felt so absurd, he almost laughed aloud, right there in the muddy street in front of his business.

He glanced at the mountains to the west, towering over the depot and the large hotel. They seemed even more magnificent than normal, their snow-covered peaks glistening in the sunlight. In fact the day felt warmer and the air even more clear and crisp.

If all went well, he might be a married man by the end of summer. A married man with a successful business and with good standing in a new town.

Now that was something to write home about.

Chapter Two

RICHMOND, VIRGINIA—JUNE 1876

"Clara Ann Brown, you cannot be serious."

Clara peered over the edge of the newspaper at her dearest friend. Violet had such a look of disbelief that Clara almost wanted to laugh.

"No." Violet shook her head, sending the carefully curled ringlets around her face flying. She plucked the paper from Clara's hands and laid it to the side. "This is not a good solution to your problem. And your problem is hardly a problem at all! There are so many good young men here."

Clara sat back in the cushioned chair in Violet's bedroom. Like everything else in the room, it was of the latest fashion. "Name one who would marry me."

Violet stood and paced across the room, her new pink dress gliding across the floorboards. "George Bartlett. I saw him watching you at our dinner party last weekend."

Clara tried not to pull a face. "Mr. Bartlett has a terrible habit of not listening to a word anyone else says, particularly if that person is a lady. Besides, he is only interested in women of means."

"Yes," Violet said, frowning. She brightened again immediately. "Matthew Voyles. You know he's entered into business with Mr. Betton? He ought to do well."

"Mr. Voyles is nearly twice our age!"

"You said nothing about age, Clara." Violet fixed her with a look of annoyance.

Clara sat forward in her chair. "Just because Gideon decided . . ." She bit down on her lip. His betrayal still hurt, even after all these months. She swallowed and looked up at her friend. "That doesn't mean I'm willing to be married to an old man."

"Mr. Voyles is hardly old, but all right." Violet sat again on the bed beside Clara's chair and took her hand. Despite her desire to see Clara married to any number of unsuitable matches, Clara knew Violet had only her best interests at heart. No one else had been such a comfort to Clara after Gideon had broken off their engagement. Violet had visited daily, sitting with her for hours. When Clara wanted to talk of her heartbreak, Violet listened. And when she wished to be distracted from the sadness that had seemed to infiltrate every aspect of her life, Violet regaled her with gossip and silly memories and the tales of New York City her brother had written her.

Clara couldn't ask for a better friend, even if that friend was now trying to persuade her to remain in Richmond.

"Roy Collins?"

"He would marry you, but not me." Clara didn't add that the only reason she knew many of the men Violet named was because she was Violet's friend. Clara's family was hardly in the same social circles as Violet's.

"Henry North?"

"He's duller than . . . than . . ." In fact, Clara couldn't think of anything duller than Mr. North.

"What about Christopher Avery? You know him well."

"Well enough to know that he's been in love with Alexandra since we were children," Clara said with a slight smile. Poor Christopher was so smitten with Alexandra, he would never have eyes for anyone else.

Violet sighed audibly. "Well, I don't understand why you feel the need to write to a stranger. And one so far away! Why don't I ask my father if you can accompany me to New York to visit with Peter? Surely my brother can introduce us to any number of good, eligible men there."

"New York is so far away, it might as well be the Colorado Territory," Clara said pointedly.

"It's not the same! Clara, I'd be sick with worry if you went out there to meet some man you've never seen. In fact, I'd likely *die* of worry. You wouldn't want that to happen, would you? My father would complain about the high expense of my funeral."

Clara giggled. "Of course not."

"So you won't write to this man, will you?"

Clara stood and retrieved the marriage newspaper from Violet's dressing table. She'd been purchasing these papers for nearly two months, in secret. At first, it was on a whim, just to see what might be inside, what sort of men might be so in need of wives they'd pay to place an advertisement. She read them with curiosity, not really taking any of them seriously.

But something had changed in the last couple of weeks. She'd begun reading them more in earnest, visions of snow-capped mountains and arid deserts and wide plains dancing in her mind. She wondered if she was brave enough to take such a chance. Could she, Clara Brown, a girl born and raised in genteel Richmond, to a solid family that wasn't as wealthy as Violet's but which provided well enough for Clara and her younger siblings, board a train headed for such a wild part of the country to possibly marry a man she'd never laid eyes on?

It had become almost a challenge of sorts. She'd read the advertisements, debating whether the various men were worthy of such a chance. But when she was honest with herself, none of them were.

Until today.

Clara unfolded the paper again. She'd purchased the one she usually bought, but this week, there had been a new paper. It was only one page in length, printed front and back, and titled *The Fremont County Marriage Advertiser*. According to the note at the top of the paper, all the men wanting wives in this paper were from one area of the Colorado Territory. But what had caught her eye in the store was this line:

Proprietresses: Mrs. Jacob Gilbert and Mrs. Benjamin Young, dedicated to publishing advertisements only from men of quality.

Clara didn't know the first thing about Mrs. Gilbert or Mrs. Young, but she figured two women would know more about what a lady might like in a husband than a man. The part about "men of quality" was also quite reassuring. She handed the paper to Violet and pointed to that line.

"But what if your standard of a marriageable man is different from theirs?" Violet asked.

"It may be," Clara replied. "But I don't *have* to marry him if I arrive and find I don't care for him."

"Hmm." Violet was studying the advertisement that had finally persuaded Clara that this was what she wanted. After a moment, she raised her eyes. "I suppose he doesn't sound too terrible."

Clara's heart lifted. Was it possible Violet saw the possibility Clara did? She sat beside her friend and gazed at the advertisement.

"I like that he owns a livery," Clara said. "A man who cares for horses must surely also care for people. And look, he speaks of his family. He must have a good background. He sounds hardworking and smart and—"

"Handsome," Violet supplied with a slight smile.

Clara's cheeks warmed. "Well, yes. That too." The man had described himself as dark-haired with brown eyes, tall, and aged twenty-seven years old. Entirely the opposite of Gideon Maxwell, the man that until a few months ago, she'd thought she'd marry.

Violet set the paper aside and took Clara's hands in her own. "You're my oldest and dearest friend. Selfishly, I can't imagine you not being here. Who will I tell first when I finally decide which beau I like best?"

Clara laughed. Violet had so many more prospects with her standing in Richmond society. Clara might have options too, if she'd let herself look. The men who worked with her father had sons. But it was hard to consider that when it seemed everywhere she went, Gideon was there with his new bride.

Sometimes she felt as if she couldn't breathe in Richmond. As if everyone was watching her and pitying her. Starting anew somewhere far from here was best. And the more she'd pondered it, the more she yearned for it—a new beginning, an adventure, and all of the possibilities a place like the Colorado Territory might hold for her.

Violet sighed. "If you feel so deeply that you ought to write to this man and see what he has to offer, I believe you should. Who knows? He may make you unbelievably happy! Or as happy as you can be without me."

Emotions pulled at every corner of Clara's heart. She threw her arms around Violet. "You don't know how much your approval means to me. I'll write him. But please promise me one thing."

"What is that?" Violet asked.

"Will you assist me in telling my parents?"

Violet's eyes widened. "All right. But only because I know you'd do the same for me. Come, I'll help you write the letter to your future husband. What should we tell him about first? Your great beauty? Your incomparable talent at everything you attempt? Or maybe your insurmountable charm?"

Clara laughed as Violet led the way to the door. But as she followed her friend to the drawing room, she wondered what might make Mr. Roman Carlisle choose her, of all the women who might write to him?

Chapter Three

ROMAN WINCED AS HE patted the handkerchief over the cut on his chin. It was a fool thing, deciding to shave at the very last minute. But he'd caught a glimpse of himself in one of the livery windows, and that had made up his mind. Truth be told, he didn't know if Miss Brown had a preference for or against whiskers, but she came from a city and he worried that the beard made him look too rough.

"You look like you lost a fight with a bear," Jeremiah said from the doorway. He'd propped himself up against the frame while Roman sat behind the stable, next to the corral that stretched out until it reached the frame of the house he'd started building.

"It doesn't look that bad," Roman said. He pulled the handkerchief away to check his reflection in the small, cloudy mirror again. The cut was noticeable, but not terrible.

"I thought beards and such were fashionable back East," Jeremiah added unhelpfully.

Roman glared at him. "What do you know about what's in fashion anywhere?"

His friend threw up his hands. "Just trying to say I doubt the lady cares one way or the other. If she's worth anything, anyhow."

Roman turned his glower onto his own reflection. Jeremiah was right, but he was determined to make a good first impression.

"Train's been at the depot now for a quarter of an hour," Jeremiah said. "Want me to fetch her for you?"

"No. Wait, it's been—what?" Roman yanked the watch from his trousers pocket. Sure enough, it was already a quarter after twelve. How had he missed the whistle? He must've been inside, or far too intent on his shaving.

He quickly cleaned up. It was the height of summer in the valley, with the sun warm enough during the day that he certainly didn't need a heavy coat. Although after glancing down at his Sunday best, Roman almost wished he could wear a coat. The trousers were more worn than he would have liked, and his jacket was beginning to fray at the seams. There was nothing to be done about it now, however. All he could hope was that Jeremiah was right, and Miss Brown would reserve her judgment until she came to know him.

Roman shoved his hat on as he sped through the stable. Only a couple of horses remained inside, the others turned out in the corral. He emerged from the front of the stable to find the waiting train sitting on the tracks that stretched through the middle of the burgeoning town. The cars hid the depot from his sight. He walked quickly south, until he was far enough that he could make his way around the idling engine. He leapt up onto the platform, his heart racing as if he'd just galloped into town on an unbroken horse. A few folks milled about. Many were up at the hotel, enjoying a quick noon meal before reboarding the train, while those who planned to remain in Crest Stone had already made their way into town.

Miss Brown had described herself as having fair hair and being of a taller stature for a lady. No one on the platform appeared to match that description. Roman's nerves melted into a sense of dread. Had she changed her mind and remained in Virginia? Had something happened to her on her journey here?

He pushed open the door to the depot. Only one lady sat inside, and she appeared much older than Miss Brown's twenty-one years.

"Good afternoon, Carlisle," Lawrence Thomason, the town's railroad clerk, postmaster, and telegraph operator said from behind his window. "Got a letter to mail home?" The older fellow's eyes took in Roman's nicest suit with curiosity.

Roman tugged on the hem of his vest, feeling ten sorts of uncomfortable. "I don't suppose you've seen a young lady asking for me?"

"I haven't," Thomason said, in voice that clearly wanted to know more.

Roman nodded his thanks and returned outside. He stood on the platform, searching around him. The train blocked the view of the northeast of town, where his livery stood. To the south and southeast, along the tracks, Crest Stone stretched out, a mix of finished and unfinished buildings and people moving about, the dark Wet Mountains far to the east behind them. In just the few months he'd been here, the town seemed to have quadrupled in population. Behind the depot, the Crest Stone Hotel sat like a throne upon a hill, the jagged Sangre de Cristo mountains piercing the sky behind it.

Could she have followed the other passengers up to the hotel? Or perhaps she'd gone in search of a boardinghouse. If she was here at all, that was. Roman sighed in frustration. If only he'd arrived at the depot before the train, at least he'd know for certain whether she was in Crest Stone.

He took off his hat, slapped it against his thigh, and then stepped forward decisively.

But after an hour of searching the hotel's restaurant and lunch counter, walking through town, and inquiring at the boardinghouse, Roman still hadn't found Miss Brown or anyone who knew anything about her. And that meant only one thing.

She hadn't bothered coming.

Perhaps she'd fallen ill. Or maybe something had delayed her and she'd be on a later train. Roman brushed aside the pesky bits of hope that circled his mind. He was clutching fast to something that wasn't going to happen.

The thought that she'd given up on him before even meeting him weighed heavily on Roman's heart. What was wrong with him? His brothers certainly had no problems following the right path, doing work his parents could be proud of, marrying good women, having children, and leading lives of worth. Why was such a thing so impossible for him?

By the time he reached the livery, Roman was in a black mood. If he'd still been a drinking man, he would have turned and made his way to the half-built saloon that was already keeping the men in town well liquored up. But he'd given that up long ago, and so the only solution to making it through the shame and sadness and irritation that lurked about him now was to work harder. He'd already pulled off his jacket, thinking he'd tackle building the wagon first. The one he owned was rented out most days already; a second would bring in additional income. He'd already purchased the wheels and the lumber, all of it waiting in the lean-to behind the stable.

He tossed the jacket into the back room where he lived with Jeremiah, not bothering to change into clothing more suited to work. The quicker he dove into something to occupy his mind, the sooner his mood would lift. And, hopefully, the faster he'd forget about Miss Brown's rejection. He couldn't fathom reading back through the other letters he'd received, not yet anyway. Not a one of those ladies had caught his attention the way Miss Brown had.

Or perhaps he was doomed to be a bachelor the rest of his days. Maybe he deserved just that.

The large barn doors at both the front and rear of the stable were open, but Roman opted for the smaller door near the back room. He shoved it open harder than he meant. The door hit the outside wall with a bang. A distinctly female shriek sounded from the right, where he'd been shaving earlier. Roman stopped short, the door wide open.

And there, sitting on one of the only three chairs he and Jeremiah owned, a lady stared at him, her green eyes wide with fright and a hand resting over her heart. The woman was like a ray of sunshine, sent to chase away his cloudy thoughts. Her hair was the color of creamy butter, she wore a dress in shades of green, and her face was sweet and round, as if she'd never seen anything distressing in her life.

Roman stood there and blinked at her. He barely noticed the door hitting his shoulder.

Jeremiah stood from where he sat next to the woman. "Miss Brown, meet Roman Carlisle. Your intended, if I'm not mistaken."

Chapter Four

CLARA COULD HARDLY breathe. Between the sudden slamming of the livery door and the tall man who stood just feet away from her, it was as if she had forgotten how to draw in air.

She somehow managed to stand as Mr. Wiley, the affable man who'd greeted her upon her arrival to Carlisle's Livery, pulled on his hat and walked toward his boss.

"And now if you'll excuse me, I believe I need to see to . . . something." Mr. Wiley grinned at Mr. Carlisle, as if the entire situation amused him, before pressing past and disappearing into the stable.

Clara twisted her gloved hands together as Mr. Carlisle's eyes found her again. The way he'd looked at her when he first saw her was unexpected. And now he looked at her that way again—curiosity and surprise mixed with something else . . . She'd seen that look a few times before, mostly from Gideon before he'd grown tired of her and turned his attentions elsewhere. It was like something barely contained, and unlike Violet, Clara never quite knew how to react.

"Pardon me, I . . ." Mr. Carlisle finally removed his hat and took a few steps toward her, letting the door close behind him. He cleared his throat again and pulled at the worn gray vest he

19

wore. "I'd gone looking for you. I didn't find you, and I thought . . ." He shook his head, as if chasing the words away.

He stopped in front of her, a good few inches taller, to Clara's everlasting relief considering her own height. She forced herself to look up at him and offer a friendly smile, even as the nerves made her want to start giggling uncontrollably. Up close, he was even more handsome, with hair so dark it rivaled the night sky. Clara tried not to think about how nice he looked in his shirt and vest, but it was clear he worked hard for a living. His warm brown eyes held her gaze, and she noticed the small scar above his lips and the more recent cut nearby.

One thing was for certain: Mr. Carlisle's advertisement had not done him justice. Clara would certainly have something to write about to Violet.

"I feared you'd forgotten my arrival date," Clara said, her voice shaking some. She paused, swallowing and trying to steady her breathing under the intense look he pressed upon her. She'd hardly been as outgoing as Violet at home, but she'd never thought of herself as a wilting flower. So she pushed her shoulders back and kept her eyes on his. "I thought I'd come find your place of business."

"And you did," he said, not moving an inch.

"I did." What was she supposed to say now? She could hardly piece two thoughts together with the way he held her eyes. In fact, she thought she might forget how to stand entirely if he kept this up.

He finally seemed to realize he'd been staring at her and looked away, rubbing a hand over his chin. "I . . . uh . . . I'm glad you arrived safely."

Clara brightened at the memory of her journey westward. "It was long and tiring and sooty, but—oh!—I saw *so* many fascinating places and people. The mountains in Virginia and Kentucky, and the wide, wide length of the plains, all of the rivers, and I could *never* have imagined the mountains here! I'd do it all again, if I could." She'd spent most of the trip with her eyes locked on what was outside the window. And when they stopped at various towns and cities, her fascination was fastened upon those who walked up and down the depot platforms and boarded the train. Businessmen and traveling salesmen, ladies dressed in finery, cowboys, and people so impoverished Clara could hardly imagine their circumstances.

Mr. Carlisle looked at her as if she'd completely lost touch with her senses, and then he smiled. "I can't say I've ever heard a woman carry on so about days spent on a train."

"I do thank you for the funds you paid for my travels. I . . ." Clara paused, realizing she had no idea what should come next. Surely he didn't expect her to marry him right away, did he? Did she want him to? If she did wish for that, she'd be quite the ninny. After all, who married a man she only just met?

And yet, some wild part of her hoped he just might suggest such a thing.

Mr. Carlisle shifted his stance, clasping his hands behind his back. "You're welcome." He paused, looking everywhere but at her. Finally, he raised his eyes, appearing so uncomfortable Clara wished she could take his hand and reassure him all would be well.

"I must confess I don't entirely know how this works," he said. "But I thought it would be ideal if we took time to get to know one another first, before . . . well . . ."

"Yes, I agree," Clara replied. But even as she felt herself relax, a disappointment crept into her thoughts. She pressed her lips together and forced it away.

"There is a boardinghouse in town, only just built. I thought you might like to stay there. I can set you up." He paused. "Unless you prefer the hotel?"

"Oh, no, the boardinghouse is just fine." Clara couldn't imagine sleeping in a hotel as fine as the one standing upon the hill behind the depot. She likely wouldn't sleep as she worried about wrinkling the bedsheets.

"Good," Mr. Carlisle said, and Clara detected a hint of relief in his voice. He bent down and gathered the two carpetbags she'd brought. "You haven't a trunk?"

Clara shook her head, trying not to let her embarrassment color her face. She didn't possess one, and she could hardly have asked her father—who disapproved highly of this venture of hers—to purchase one. So she'd settled for her mother's old carpetbag and another gifted to her from Violet. They just barely fit her possessions, but she'd managed to bring enough clothing to be serviceable, and a few small mementos and items for her toilette.

But if Mr. Carlisle found it strange she'd come without a trunk full of goods, he didn't show it. In fact, he smiled as he lifted the carpetbags.

"Tomorrow I'll show you about town, if you'd like," he said.

"I'd enjoy that."

He gestured at her to go first, and so Clara entered the livery, Mr. Carlisle following with her bags. It smelled of straw and horse inside, exactly the same as the livery where Papa occasionally rented a carriage and horses. She breathed it in, and it gave her courage. How strange to come such a distance, only to find something that reminded her so easily of home.

Mr. Wiley stood just inside the big door that led to the street, speaking with a man holding the reins of a horse. The man was dusty and wore clothing that looked as if it had seen numerous days of hard travel in the saddle. He glanced at Clara, his eyes lingering on her a moment too long, and not leaving until Mr. Carlisle paused beside her.

Clara swallowed hard, and, ignoring the strange man, turned to Mr. Wiley. "Thank you again, Mr. Wiley, for entertaining me this afternoon."

"It was my pleasure, miss," he said, pulling on his hat.

"I'll return in a while," Mr. Carlisle said, his eyes on the dusty man even as he spoke to Mr. Wiley.

Mr. Wiley nodded, and Mr. Carlisle pulled the smaller door open for Clara. She escaped through it, back into the warm sunlight and away from the chill that stranger had brought.

Too many men have been too long without women in the territories, her father had said, ignoring the fact that Colorado would soon likely be a state. At the time, it made no sense. After all, wasn't that exactly why men such as Mr. Carlisle were placing advertisements for brides? But now that she was here, and she'd seen the look in that man's eyes, her father's words took on a different meaning. Even Violet, as supportive as she was, asked Clara if she oughtn't learn to shoot a pistol before leaving home. Clara had laughed those concerns away, certain Violet had read one too many dime novels about outlaws and Indians. But now . . . perhaps she should have taken her friend's worry seriously.

"The boardinghouse is safe," Mr. Carlisle said, seeming to know her exact thoughts. "It's run by a gentleman and his sister who came from somewhere in Minnesota, I think. Or Wisconsin?" He shook his head. "They don't rent rooms to people of questionable character."

Clara wondered where the folks of questionable character slept, but that felt like an odd question to ask.

They crossed the road, Clara lifting her skirts and stepping as carefully as possible. At least it wasn't wet. She couldn't imagine the mess this road would become in the rain or snow. Mr. Carlisle led her across the railroad tracks and past the depot. They passed several partially built structures and newly constructed buildings, including—to Clara's delight—what appeared to be a church. Farther down the road, men called loudly to each other from within a saloon missing three of its four walls.

The last building they reached was completed, and a large painted sign above the door declared it to be Darby's Boardinghouse. Mr. Carlisle pushed the door open, and Clara entered.

A cheerful parlor room met her gaze. A few chairs and a comfortable-looking settee sat positioned as if for conversation. A dining room was off to the right, beyond the stairs, and from there, a woman just slightly older than Clara, with a plain face and hair as black as a crow's wing, came bustling in.

"Good afternoon, Miss Darby," Mr. Carlisle said. He set the carpetbags down and removed his hat.

"Mr. Carlisle," she said in return, even as her friendly but curious eyes flicked back to Clara.

"May I introduce Miss Brown? Miss Brown, this is Miss Darby, the proprietress of this boardinghouse."

The two ladies nodded at each other and exchanged pleasantries.

"I assume you're in need of a room?" Miss Darby asked, glancing at Clara's carpetbags.

"I am, thank you," Clara replied.

"I'll be taking care of the bill," Mr. Carlisle said.

His words made Miss Darby's eyebrows raise. Clara wanted to protest, to assure him that was unnecessary, but the truth was, she had little in the way of funds to pay for more than a few nights. And most of that money had been a gift from Violet, hidden inside the carpetbag she'd given Clara.

"Then I'll ready the room." Miss Darby swept upstairs to presumably do just that.

"Thank you, Mr. Carlisle," Clara said, as soon as Miss Darby was out of earshot. "I would offer to—"

"It's no bother," he said, straightening. "You are my responsibility."

Responsibility. The word made her sound as if she were one of his horses, in need of grooming and feeding. She'd come here to be his wife, not his *responsibility.* Unless . . . Had he already changed his mind about her, just as Gideon had?

Clara tried in vain not to fidget as the fear of rejection raced through her. Mr. Carlisle replaced his hat, as if readying to leave.

"I can carry those bags up, if you'd like," he said.

"It's quite all right," she replied. "I can manage. Thank you." She kept her shoulders straight and her chin up. If he wanted to leave her so badly, she wouldn't try to make him stay.

"I'll see you tomorrow, Miss Brown." He nodded and was out the door so quickly, Clara barely had time to register his disappearance.

The moment the door closed, she slumped against the wall. Not only had he called her a responsibility, he had left so abruptly. He hadn't asked her to call him by his given name either. If she was to marry him, shouldn't they be on more familiar terms? And speaking of marriage . . . Why was he putting it off?

Something was wrong with her. She knew it deep down inside. It couldn't be her appearance. After all, she'd managed to keep Gideon's interest for nigh on eight months. And Mr. Carlisle hadn't seemed disgusted when he saw her. It had to be some defect in her demeanor or her personality. Something that drove men away. But what?

Clara pressed a hand to her stomach, which knotted in disappointment and shame.

He *had* said he'd see her tomorrow. If he was so uninterested in her, wouldn't he ask Mr. Wiley to see her off to the depot, rather than paying for her to stay at this boardinghouse and making plans to visit with her the next day?

She pulled in a deep breath. Somewhere in the rear of the boardinghouse, someone was cooking meat. The scent of it made her stomach growl. She hadn't had anything truly worth eating since she'd left Virginia. And her body ached with the days and days of jostling travel on the train.

Perhaps she was just hungry and tired. That must be fraying her nerves and making her read far too much into Mr. Carlisle's words and actions. After all, she hardly knew the man. She knew only what they'd exchanged in two letters each.

Perhaps he had somewhere to be, or he didn't fully trust Mr. Wiley to tend to the livery. And some men weren't particularly good with words. Maybe Mr. Carlisle was one of them.

Now that her nerves had calmed some, Clara almost wanted to laugh at herself. If Violet were here, she'd tell Clara she was being ridiculous and under no circumstances should she want to marry Mr. Carlisle before getting to know him better. He likely felt the same way.

It would be fine. It *had* to be fine.

Else she'd find herself returning home in shame, to a life of dreary and almost certain spinsterhood with no adventure ever to be had at all.

Chapter Five

ROMAN HAD JUST BLINKED the sleep from his eyes when Jeremiah's urgent voice sounded from inside the stable.

"Boss! We've got a problem!"

Roman pulled up his suspenders as he pushed through the door that led from the back room into the stable. "What is it?" he called as Jeremiah strode toward him.

"Alliance is missing." Jeremiah dragged a hand through his hair, leaving it even more unkempt than it looked before.

"That's impossible. I put him in the stall myself last night."

Jeremiah shook his head. "I'm telling you, he ain't there now."

Roman wrinkled his forehead. Had he put the horse in the wrong stall? He jogged past Jeremiah, toward where Alliance normally spent the night in a stall near the front of the stable.

It was empty.

"I checked every stall and the corral. He's not here," Jeremiah said from behind him.

Roman rubbed his hands across his face. "That can't be." Alliance was one of his horses, purchased expressly to rent out from the livery. He looked down the rest of the stalls. Every other horse appeared accounted for, including his own Thunder.

"Maybe Granger came in early for him," Roman said. Granger rented out Alliance a couple times each week to pull wagon loads of timber from Silver Creek.

"Can't be. He didn't take lines or a harness." Jeremiah looked as if he wanted to say more, but didn't.

"If you've got something to say, say it." Roman wanted to hear something—anything—that disputed the notion that someone had waltzed into his stable at some point during the night and made off with one of his horses. All while both he and Jeremiah were fast asleep in the back room.

"About three a.m. or so, I was up," Jeremiah said, looking vaguely uncomfortable. "I went out front to smoke, and Mitchell Turley came on by, drunker than a man on his last day. He was going on about needing a horse. I moved him on, but . . ."

Roman closed his eyes. While Jeremiah was distracted with Turley, anyone could've come in and helped himself to Alliance.

"I had to walk him down the road a ways. If someone led Alliance out, it could be I didn't see him."

Roman drew in a deep breath, steadying the irritation that rolled through him. Jeremiah was a good friend. He'd been there from the start, when Roman rode into Crest Stone with nothing but a couple of horses, a few dollars, and a big idea. "It's not your fault," he said finally.

Jeremiah's shoulders seemed to sag in relief.

"If you can take care of everything here, I'll go on and see Wright." The fellow who'd taken Alliance had likely left town right away, but it was still worth letting the newly elected marshal—the only law in town—know what had happened.

Jeremiah nodded, and Roman returned quickly to the back room to finish dressing. The apparent theft of Alliance weighed heavily on his mind. New people came into Crest Stone every day. If word got around that his livery was easy pickings for desperate men, he'd be out of business before he'd barely started it.

The sun was just rising over the tops of the Wet Mountains to the east when he left, and the town was still quiet. He made his way across the railroad tracks, down to the depot, and then up the hill to the hotel. Crest Stone's marshal had no office or home yet; both were still under construction. Roman hoped it was early enough the man hadn't left the hotel to make his rounds or see to any other business. He'd sent word to Miss Brown late yesterday that he'd see her at noon for a meal and a tour of the town. Which meant he had little time to make this errand to see Marshal Wright and still accomplish what he needed back at the livery.

Miss Brown. Her round, pretty face filled his mind as he climbed the hill to the hotel. She was far more attractive than he could have ever imagined. And had a sweet disposition, too, with a kind smile and a sunny outlook.

You don't deserve her.

Roman bit down on the thought—the same one that had sent him running yesterday from the boardinghouse. It didn't matter that he'd frittered away the past ten years, driving cattle and working as a ranch hand, only to spend most of what he made in saloons. He was different now, finally able to look to the future. He had a business and men like Jake Gilbert and Marshal Wright treated him like an equal. He was on the verge of having everything he wanted, so long as he didn't give in to his doubts.

The desk clerk at the Crest Stone Hotel pointed Roman down a hallway that ran past the grand staircase. The place never failed to draw a moment of awe from Roman, with its soaring ceiling and two enormous stone fireplaces, warding off the morning's chill.

Roman paused in front of the door the clerk had directed him to. It was open, and it appeared to be set up as an office. Just inside, Wright sat behind a fine wooden desk. Roman breathed out, glad he wouldn't be waking the man from his slumber. The marshal looked up from what he was writing and gestured at Roman to come inside. Roman imagined Wright's job had gotten somewhat easier since he'd recently cleared the town of a couple of outlaw gangs from Kansas—one of which Roman had heard the marshal's wife was related to.

"Good to see you, Carlisle," Wright said as he stood and made his way around the desk.

Roman took his proffered hand. "Morning, Marshal. Wish it was under better circumstances."

Wright's usually serious face grew more concerned. "What happened?"

Roman told him of the missing horse and about how the culprit might have stolen Alliance while Jeremiah was distracted.

"I'll have a talk with Mitchell Turley," Wright said when Roman finished. "See what he knows."

"Doubt he knows much. Jeremiah said he was in his usual nightly state."

"Could be, but the timing seems awfully convenient to me."

Roman nodded, wondering why that hadn't occurred to him too. He thanked Wright and made his way back to the livery.

The morning flew by, with customers in and out, tracking down a fellow whose horse had thrown a shoe, buying vegetables from the hotel stables because his own order had been delayed, and fixing one of the wheels on the wagon just in time for the men finishing up a couple of houses to rent it for the day, along with the numerous other tasks and responsibilities that came with caring for horses and running a business. As soon as he could afford it, Roman determined he'd hire someone else. Most days, it was almost too much work for just him and Jeremiah. Occasionally, a man down on his luck but needing to stable his horse would offer to work in exchange, but it had been a solid two weeks since they'd had that sort of help.

When his grumbling stomach caused him to pull out his pocket watch, Roman discovered he was supposed to meet Miss Brown in five minutes. He'd be late again.

He let out a frustrated sigh and walked quickly back to wash up and change into something that didn't smell of straw and manure. She'd been forgiving of his misstep yesterday. He could only hope that she'd do the same today.

Roman stepped out of the livery ten minutes later, halfway convinced Miss Brown would demand to return to Virginia. Surely there were any number of men there who could keep their word and meet her at the time they'd promised. He passed the depot, nodding at young Christopher Rennet, who assisted Thomason with running telegrams about town and selling tickets to Denver and Santa Fe. Just as he passed the church, someone called his name.

Roman turned and spotted Marshal Wright.

"Glad I caught you," Wright said as he approached.

Roman paused, torn between wishing he could turn back the hands of the clock and wanting to hear what Wright had to tell him.

"I spoke with Turley."

"I'm surprised he wasn't still abed," Roman replied, his curiosity growing. Wright wouldn't have chased him down if he had nothing of note to share.

"Oh, he was," Wright said with a slight smile. "Anyhow, I got it out of him that someone slipped him some coins if he'd go knock on the livery door and ask for a horse."

Roman frowned. That could only mean one thing . . .

"Someone set the fool up," the marshal continued. "And stole off with your horse."

"I don't suppose he knew who the man was?"

Wright shook his head. "Couldn't tell me what he looked like either. Which is likely why the thief asked a drunk man to lure Wiley away from the livery."

The marshal bid Roman good afternoon and said he'd keep an eye out for the missing horse. Roman watched him disappear back down the road, the news still on his mind. It was pure dumb luck that Turley had found Jeremiah already awake. If he'd knocked, Roman likely would've woken too. And if he had, perhaps he'd have heard the horse thief.

It was over and done with now. It was unlikely he'd ever see Alliance again. So long as the man left town, he could at least hope word wouldn't get out and lead other ill-intentioned men to attempt to help themselves to horses too.

He couldn't dwell on it now, not when he was an embarrassing twenty minutes late to meet Miss Brown. What an impression he was making.

He'd be lucky if she hadn't already purchased a ticket home.

Chapter Six

CLARA SAT IN THE SMALL parlor at the boardinghouse, trying in vain to keep worry and desperation from creeping in. He was twenty minutes late. And after being late to meet her yesterday, and then leaving so abruptly last night, there was no other conclusion she could reach save one.

His interest had already waned.

A sound from the boardinghouse's entryway made hope flicker, only to be dashed once again when she saw it was one of the gentlemen who rented a room on the ground floor. Mr. Darby, Miss Darby's sharp-eared brother, slept in a room right by the stairs, which lent comfort to the ladies staying on the second floor. And according to Miss Darby, in the two months they'd been open, he'd already thrown out a sizable number of men who couldn't keep to the rules.

The gentleman tipped his hat to her, and Clara nodded a hello before returning to ruminating on how she'd already managed to drive Mr. Carlisle away. Was she too eager to please? Too open with her enthusiasm about being here? Or was she too dull? She never knew the reason Gideon ended their engagement—only that he'd been taken with the woman he'd ended up marrying. If only he'd told her *why*. Maybe then she could have rectified that fault in her character and she wouldn't be sitting here alone, wondering why it seemed to be happening all over again.

She'd so been looking forward to an excursion around the town, too. She hadn't left the boardinghouse since she'd arrived the day before, but the people and the view out her front-facing window had her eager to see all of Crest Stone.

Yesterday, she'd walked the short distance from the depot to the livery alone. Why shouldn't she do the same now? After all, if this was Mr. Carlisle's way of rejecting her, she'd be on a train back to Virginia soon. She'd longed for adventure, to see a world beyond the one she knew, and to return home without doing any of that was too disappointing to consider.

Well, if she wasn't getting the marriage and new life she'd dreamed of on the train out here, she surely wasn't leaving without at least seeing more of the town. With that in mind, Clara stood, pulled on a pair of gloves that had seen better days, straightened her hat, and picked up her reticule. She made her way to the door, thinking she might visit the mercantile she'd spotted yesterday. She wouldn't buy anything. After all, she didn't know yet if Mr. Carlisle would pay her fare home. She hoped he might—he seemed a gentleman, even if he didn't wish to marry her. But if he didn't, she'd need every spare bit of change she had to return.

She opened the door—and stepped right into a tall, familiar figure.

Clara stopped herself with her hands on his chest, just as he took hold of her arms to steady her. "Oh! Forgive me, Mr. Carlisle. I didn't— I mean, I . . ." Heat flooded her cheeks as she realized her hands still pressed against him.

"Are you all right?" He peered down at her with a concerned gaze. His hands felt warm where they still held her arms, strong and steady.

"Yes. Yes, I'm fine," she said much too quickly. Why did she still hold her hands against him? She curved her fingers and slowly pulled them away, trying not to think about how strong and solid he felt beneath them.

He let his hands linger for a moment before letting her go. Clara let out a breath, her heart beating so fast she feared he could hear it. What was wrong with her? Gideon had taken her hand before, and that had never caused her to be unable to think, much less breathe. Then again, Gideon's grip had never been so powerful and reassuring.

Mr. Carlisle removed his hat, crushing the brim between his fingers as if he were angry with it. But his expression wasn't angry at all. In fact, his forehead wrinkled just so, as if something worried him. "I apologize for my tardiness once again. I hadn't meant . . . Please know it was unintentional."

"Oh . . . All right." Clara didn't know what else to say. Did that mean he wanted her to stay? And after she'd just about convinced herself this wasn't meant to be!

"I thought we might take a stroll around the town, and then perhaps stop for a late lunch?" Mr. Carlisle smiled, but it was restrained, as if something still bothered him.

Clara nodded her assent. If he was still undecided about her, she'd try her best to rectify that during their time together. Of course, he'd need to prove he was worth *her* time, too. She refused to marry someone who didn't care for her.

Mr. Carlisle held the door open for her, and Clara swept through it, her head held high. They were quiet as she walked alongside him toward the center of town.

"I feel as if I should apologize again," he said out of nowhere.

Clara glanced up at him. He held his jaw tight even as he gave her a smile. Something was on his mind, and Clara couldn't tell if it concerned her or not. Well, if she wanted to know the truth about whether he wanted her to stay, she might as well find out now.

"To be honest, I feared you had changed your mind about me." Clara's throat was dry and she almost couldn't believe she'd spoken the words aloud.

But she was glad she had.

Mr. Carlisle paused in front of an empty lot beside the partially built saloon. Those dark eyes caught hers, intense . . . but with something else behind them. Worry, perhaps? Or was it fear? Clara couldn't tell, but it was hard to keep her thoughts in motion when he looked at her in that way.

"I have not," he said.

Clara's breath caught in her throat. He wasn't sending her home! *But why had he acted so disinterested?*

She wanted to shake the thought away, but it persisted. She couldn't fall into another situation like the one she'd experienced with Gideon. Her heart couldn't take that pain again.

"I am sorry if I made you think that was how I felt," Mr. Carlisle went on. He took hold of her elbow and led her a few steps away from the road, into the dirt and trampled grass of the empty lot, as two fellows carrying a long cut piece of wood passed by.

Clara clasped her hands together, feeling much braver now that he'd told her he didn't wish for her to leave. "You left so abruptly last night, and then you came late today . . . and, well . . . It appears you have something on your mind. I thought it might be something to do with me."

He pressed his lips together and gazed out across the road, where the railroad tracks sat empty while men worked hard on a building on the other side. Then he abruptly turned his eyes back to her.

"One of my horses was stolen last night," he said. "I spent part of the morning talking with the marshal."

Clara raised a hand to her mouth. "That's terrible. Do you know who took the horse?"

He shook his head. "All Marshal Wright could figure out was that a man paid off a fellow who was, well . . . inebriated—"

Clara bit her lip. It was sweet the way he went a bit red mentioning the man's unseemly state to her.

"Paid him to distract Jeremiah while he snuck in and took Alliance. The horse," he added at Clara's quizzical look.

"That seems very thought out," she said after a moment. "As if someone spent some time planning the best way to execute the theft."

Mr. Carlisle blinked at her in surprise. "Yes, I suppose it does."

"This is such a small town. I doubt the man would stay. Your horse would be too easy to recognize."

"Yes." He gave her an incredulous look.

"I wonder if he'll return," Clara mused. "It could be he only wanted the horse to leave town, in which case he won't be back.

Or it could have been a test of sorts, to see if he could get away with taking one horse."

He drew in a deep breath. "That is my greatest fear."

Clara nodded. It was a terrifying thought.

"I didn't expect you to take such an interest in my business," he said with a little smile.

"Oh, I . . . well . . ." Clara let the words drift into the warm summer breeze that fluttered her skirts.

"I'm glad you do."

Clara swallowed. He was looking at her as if she were a puzzle that fascinated him. "I like horses," she said, for lack of anything better to say.

"As do I." It was an obvious statement, considering he'd based his entire livelihood around the animals. It was clear he was waiting to hear more.

"And I thought, well . . ." She could feel her cheeks going pink, and she looked at the ground. "I thought that if I was to be your wife, I ought to have an interest in your stable."

When he didn't say anything, she looked up. He'd taken off his hat, and was turning it around in his hands, as if he were deep in thought.

"Miss Brown," he said suddenly. "I don't suppose you might be interested in helping at the livery? Not with cleaning out stalls or anything like that, but perhaps assisting with customers? Jeremiah and I have more work than we can handle most days."

A happy warmth flooded Clara from head to toe. Not only did he want her here, he needed her assistance. "I would love to help."

He grinned, wider than she'd seen since she met him. "Good. Thank you." He replaced his hat and held out an arm. "Shall we tour the rest of the town, and then take some lunch? I hear Miss Darby's ham and bean soup is the best for miles around."

Clara giggled and took his arm. "There isn't much of anything for miles around."

"Well, I fear it's that or Jeremiah's cold beans from last night," he said with a look on his face that indicated she'd much prefer the soup.

He led her about the little town, pointing out various places of interest. There wasn't much to it, not yet. The main road was split in two, lining each side of the railroad tracks. The beginnings of what might become side roads that ran from west to east sat between a few buildings on the east side of the tracks. The hotel upon its hill took up most of the land to the west, and behind that, Mr. Carlisle told her, Silver Creek ran along the base of the towering Sangre de Cristo mountains.

Clara found her gaze wandering to the mountains again and again. They were beautiful and forbidding at the same time, topped with snow at their peaks, and watching over the town like ancient sentinels. The lower, dark Wet Mountains far to the east of the valley were farther away and home to a mining encampment, Mr. Carlisle said.

They visited the general store and mercantile, admired the smithy's work, and perused a few half-finished buildings. Mr. Carlisle pointed out the church, the bank, and other buildings of note. After lunch at the boardinghouse, he promised to return early the next morning to bring her to the livery.

Clara wrote two quick letters—one to her parents and the other to Violet—letting them know she'd arrived safely and met Mr. Carlisle. She hesitated to say more about him just yet. Although the way he'd acted today gave her no reason to doubt him, she almost feared putting her hopes into words. She wanted so badly to trust him, but it was difficult to let her guard down entirely.

After supper that evening and conversation with the two other ladies staying at the boardinghouse, Clara climbed into bed with a contented sigh and smiled at the ceiling. The town was mostly silent outside her window, save for a shout or two from men visiting the saloon down the road. She felt a world away from home, in this remote place where the only souls she knew were people she'd met yesterday.

But it was all so exciting! Now that she was here, now that she'd seen the soaring mountains and the expansive wilderness, the rough men and brave women who dared to live in such a place, she couldn't imagine returning to her staid, safe life in Virginia.

She prayed that Mr. Carlisle would be nothing like Gideon, that he'd continue to find her interesting, and that he'd appreciate her help at the livery tomorrow. And then she drifted off, dreaming of a wedding in the new little church, a dark-haired, hardworking man standing beside her, pledging to love and protect her for always.

Chapter Seven

ROMAN WAS UP BEFORE dawn, full of a restless energy that made him want to accomplish everything all at once. It was far too early to fetch Miss Brown, much to his disappointment. By the time Jeremiah arose, Roman had already fed the horses and turned them out to the corral.

He set to work mucking out a stall, but his mind wasn't on the day's chores or the empty stall nearby that Alliance had once occupied. Instead, his thoughts kept turning toward a smile that could light up a room and hair that seemed made of sunlight itself. If he'd been surprised that Miss Brown had taken an interest in the livery, he was even more impressed at her shrewd mind. Miss Clara Brown was not just pretty, but smart too.

She'd be an asset to the livery, he thought. With her friendly disposition and the easy way she seemed to get along with everyone she met, from Jeremiah to Miss Darby to the townsfolk he'd introduced her to in the mercantile, it would be good to have her greeting customers and helping them obtain what they needed. He imagined she'd be a quick learner too. It wouldn't be long before she knew the place inside and out.

It seemed almost too good to be true—a beautiful and kind woman he'd never met, traveling clear out here with the intention of marrying him, and wanting to be part of his work too. Perhaps something was finally going right for him, after so many years of not having any direction at all.

He wasn't entirely certain he deserved her, but he'd do his best to prove himself.

Spurred on by his optimism, he'd found a spare few minutes to lay out the wood he intended to build into a new wagon. He was no wainwright, but it would be serviceable enough to rent out. With the money he'd make, he could save up to pay someone else to make a third. He envisioned needing to add another barn, one big enough to house a collection of wagons and carriages for hire.

But first, he needed to put this one together. He cut and hammered as men who boarded their horses came in and out of the stable to the corral. It was a few minutes past nine when Jeremiah stuck his head out the door.

"You've got a visitor, Boss," he said, grinning.

Roman set down the saw and wiped his forehead with his sleeve. The chill was just starting to seep out of the morning. He followed Jeremiah back through the stable and spotted Miss Brown waiting near one of the horse stalls. She'd leaned over the stall door and was stroking the horse's nose. Roman recognized the animal. Tartan was a chestnut gelding that belonged to the banker. The banker was a big fellow, a former miner who was rough around the edges. He boarded a couple of horses and a carriage, and as he had today, he usually sent word ahead of his arrival when he needed one of the horses. Roman had yet to see the man ever use the carriage.

"He's such a beautiful horse," Miss Brown said, turning her dazzling smile to him. "What's he called?"

Roman blinked, rendered temporarily mute by how beautiful she looked this morning. She wore a light blue dress that reminded him of the sky on a clear day with a darker blue hat. The ensemble—or maybe it was the dim light in the stable—made her eyes look more gray than they had yesterday.

"The horse?" she prompted.

Roman cleared his throat, looking to the horse to clear his mind. "Tartan. He's the banker's horse." He paused. "I was coming to fetch you in about an hour."

"It's all right. I awoke early and was eager to see your stable." Miss Brown rubbed the white blaze on Tartan's nose. The horse snuffled in return and she laughed.

Jeremiah stood next to Roman, slack-jawed until Roman fixed him with a glare.

"Sorry," Jeremiah said quickly. "Just that I haven't seen a lady take to a horse in that way before. Not that I've known many ladies. Ma'am," he said to Miss Brown with a quick nod before moving quickly past her to the front of the livery.

"Please forgive Jeremiah," Roman said.

But Miss Brown didn't seem bothered. Instead, she clasped her hands together and looked about the place as if she'd never seen it before. "It's so much larger in here than it looks from outside."

Roman followed her gaze, over the stalls and the straw and dirt-covered floor. The horses were all outside, save for Tartan. He'd built the place large on purpose. "I wanted to have room to expand as the town grows."

"What do you keep back there?" Miss Brown's curious gaze was pointed at the area behind the two rows of horse stalls.

"Would you like to see?" Roman asked.

She nodded, and Roman led her past the stalls to the wide-open space beyond. Only the banker's buggy sat there, Roman's wagon having already been rented for the day.

"What a lovely carriage!" Miss Brown stood beside him, her face alight with glee.

"It belongs to the banker," Roman explained. "I have yet to see him take it out, but I suppose he's keeping it here to use at some point."

"My friend Violet's family had a buggy. I used to love riding in it about town." Miss Brown ran a hand over the conveyance's fine craftsmanship.

"One day, I hope to have a need to build another barn to keep carriages and wagons, both for boarding and for rent. Then we could build more stalls on this side of the stable." Roman could see it all in his mind—a bustling place, filled with horses and people coming and going. He'd need several more employees, of course. And perhaps then, he could afford to pay someone to sit guard all night to prevent thieves from making off with his—and his customers'—horses.

"That sounds wonderful." Miss Brown looked at him with unabashed happiness.

He grinned in response. Never had he thought she might be so interested in his plans.

"What do you keep in those rooms?" She pointed at the three closed rooms lining the rear wall of the barn.

"Tools in that one, saddles and harnesses and such in the middle one, and the other is where Jeremiah and I sleep."

She blinked at him. "You sleep in a room in the stable?"

Embarrassment crept through him. What must she think? That he intended for her to marry him and live in that room too? He pushed his shoulders back as he realized he could easily rectify that. "Follow me."

She looked at him with questions written across her face, but did as he asked.

They emerged into the bright sunlight behind the stable. The lean-to and the beginnings of the new wagon sat off to the left. To the right, closest to the smithy's shop, sat the hastily built table and chairs that served as a resting spot outside of the stable. Straight ahead, the corral stretched out with horses milling about. A few paused to look up at them. And beyond that sat the structure Roman wanted Miss Brown to see.

They moved around the corral, past where he hoped to eventually build the second barn. Nothing sat beyond it now but grass and small hills, but it would face a side road, one that already existed and headed east toward the mining camp at the base of the Wet Mountains, a few miles away. The miners mostly kept to their camp and the entertainments there, but on occasion, the distance didn't prevent them from a good time in Crest Stone, particularly since the Starlight Saloon went into business.

"What is this?" Miss Brown asked when he stopped outside the little partially built house.

"It's to be a home," he said, letting his gaze flicker to her to see her reaction.

"Oh," she said in surprise. "May I go inside?"

He nodded, and then bit down on his lip as she entered the doorframe. The place was hardly complete, but he'd already laid out each room and put a stone fireplace in the parlor. He hoped she wouldn't think it too small.

"Am I standing in the parlor?" she asked, turning to him.

Roman nodded, encouraged by her curiosity. "If you step back that way—between those pieces of wood—you'll be in the kitchen."

She did as he said and turned, looking all around her. "This is a big kitchen. Much larger than the one I grew up with."

He smiled and leaned against part of the wall's frame. He didn't know much about her circumstances in Virginia, other than that she came from a family of modest means and that her father worked as the bookkeeper for some large company. It pleased him greatly that he might be giving her more than she'd grown up with, particularly since he'd feared her life out here would be a step down from what she'd had.

If she agreed to marry him, that was.

He shoved down the fear that he couldn't possibly be enough for a woman as good as Miss Brown and tried to concentrate on how she examined what would be the kitchen, a smile playing upon her face. What was she thinking? Did she imagine herself cooking up a big dinner? Or sitting at a table and gazing out the window toward the dark mountains off in the distance? Or—

"What is this room?" Miss Brown asked, interrupting thoughts that were quickly carrying Roman away.

"That would be the bedroom."

"Oh." Her cheeks colored a pleasing pink.

Roman pushed himself up straight. "There will be a fourth room upstairs. It won't be very large, but big enough for . . ." He couldn't bring himself to say the word *children*. Somehow that seemed to be assuming too much. Although he thought he wouldn't mind seeing Miss Brown blush even more.

"Yes," she said, the pink in her cheeks deepening to a red.

"What do you think?" he asked.

"About . . . children?"

She couldn't meet his eye when she said the word, which was a good thing because he was sure he looked as scared as a newborn foal.

"No, about the house." He stood and put his hands on his hips before dropping them to his sides. How was it so hard to figure out what to do with his hands?

"I, oh, um . . ." She smiled nervously. "I love it. The house. It will be beautiful, I can tell."

Roman couldn't keep the grin from his face. "Thank you." He paused a moment. "I'm glad you like it."

She pressed a hand to one of the wooden posts. "Are you building this yourself, Mr. Carlisle?"

"I am. Please call me Roman." The moment the words were out of his mouth, he wondered if he should have spoken them. Was it too soon? But if they were getting to know each other for a potential marriage, it seemed ridiculous to go on being so formal.

"All right," she said quietly, her mouth turning up at the corners. "You may call me Clara."

"Clara," he repeated. Clara, clear as the sky. It fit her perfectly, he decided, particularly as she stood in the unfinished house with morning sunlight streaming through the wooden beams. It illuminated her hair and made her dress look as if it were made from the sky itself.

She made him forget everything he'd rather not think about, from the missing horse to whether he was even worth her attention.

When Clara smiled at him, anything seemed possible.

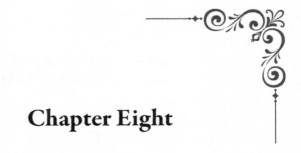

Chapter Eight

THE NEXT MORNING, CLARA left the boardinghouse early, an hour before Roman was to come get her. Her excitement had gotten the best of her yesterday, and so she'd gone to the livery early before spending a pleasant day assisting the customers. Roman hadn't seemed to mind her early arrival, but considering he told her again that he'd come escort her this morning, she figured she ought to let him.

But that didn't mean she couldn't pay a visit to the mercantile before he arrived. Miss Darby had been so kind to her since her arrival that Clara wanted to return the favor. She hoped she might find an inexpensive little trinket or something that might convey her gratitude. She dressed, ate a quick breakfast, and then made her way outside.

Clouds threatened from beyond the mountains, lending an even starker contrast to the bright green of the aspens and cottonwoods and the dark blue of the peaks. It made for such a pretty picture that Clara had a hard time drawing her gaze away and back toward the road.

The mercantile was toward the middle of town and on the opposite side of the railroad tracks. Clara picked her way across the road and the tracks, careful to avoid the manure left behind by the horses but was grateful that it hadn't rained. On her walk with Roman yesterday—it was still so strange to think of him as Roman—she'd noticed the beginnings of a board sidewalk near the depot and across the tracks by the mercantile itself. A sidewalk would make walking about town much easier, although it didn't solve the problem of crossing the road after rain. And for that, Clara was thankful that her shoes were old and sturdy, and nothing she'd need fear ruining with a bit of mud.

She made her way past rough-looking men and a handful of well-dressed gentlemen. She passed only a couple of ladies, both wearing the dove-gray dresses that Roman had told her were the uniforms of the waitresses at the hotel's restaurant. There were certainly more men in this town than women, which was somewhat disconcerting, but, she supposed, not unexpected.

Clara opened the door to the mercantile and stepped inside. Only two ladies were in the store—the one who'd been behind the counter when she visited with Roman yesterday, and another darker-haired woman with a baby in her arms. After perusing the shelves, Clara's gaze flitted to the baked goods at the counter.

She stopped beside the woman with the baby, waiting for a break in the ladies' conversation to purchase a slice of lemon cake. Just last night, Miss Darby told her how much she was looking forward to a shipment of lemons from California. Clara thought she might enjoy the slice of cake more than any little comb or figurine.

"Hello," the blonde woman with the polished voice said from behind the counter. "I'm Caroline Drexel, but please call me Caroline. I believe I saw you in here yesterday with Mr. Carlisle from the livery?"

Clara nodded. "Clara Brown," she said. "It's good to meet you, Caroline."

"This is my dear friend Emma Hartley," Caroline said, gesturing at the pretty, darker-haired woman.

"And this is Monroe," Emma said, glancing down at the baby in her arms.

"He's adorable." Clara smiled at the baby. He couldn't have been more than a month or so old.

"Thank you." Emma turned a beaming smile to Clara. "Are you new in town?"

"Yes. I've only just arrived a few days ago."

"What brings you to Crest Stone?" Caroline asked conversationally.

"I . . ." How could she explain that she'd answered a marriage advertisement? "I've come to, well . . ."

"Ohh!" Emma said, as if she'd just realized something. "Dora told me that Mr. Carlisle was one of the men who'd placed an advertisement with her service!"

"That's right!" Caroline added. Then she slapped a hand over her mouth. "Oh, Emma, that was supposed to remain quiet. Remember?"

Emma's eyes widened. "Oh, I'm so sorry, Clara. I hope we didn't embarrass you. It's only that Dora is a good friend of ours, and she was so excited when the first few men took to placing advertisements."

"It's quite all right." Clara smiled at them in relief. They didn't appear to think it was so strange that she'd come here to be a mail-order bride. In fact, they seemed happy that she helped their friend with her business.

The two ladies looked at each other, and Clara knew exactly what they wanted to ask but were too polite to do so. "We haven't married yet. We're getting to know each other."

"I see," Emma said.

"That's very smart of you," Caroline added. "Although Mr. Carlisle's only been in town for a few months, he's become a good friend to my husband."

"And mine," Emma said. "He's a builder, and your Mr. Carlisle asked him for advice when he was building the livery. And he took it to heart, which pleased my husband greatly."

"I believe Mr. Carlisle to be a good man," Caroline said.

"Of course, that's for you to decide." Emma shifted the baby to her other arm. He stretched his little hands out before pulling them back, all the while not even opening his eyes.

Clara's cheeks went warm, although she certainly was glad to hear that Roman had won the respect of these ladies and their husbands.

"I'm so sorry," Caroline said. "Did you need assistance with a purchase?"

"Oh, yes!" Clara had almost forgotten herself why she'd come into the store. "May I have a slice of that lemon cake?" She paused. "Make that three slices, if you don't mind." Surely Roman and Mr. Wiley would also appreciate a slice of cake.

"Of course. I bake them fresh each morning," Caroline replied. She cut the cake and wrapped each slice in paper, and Clara handed her some coins.

"I hope you don't mind me asking, but is it true that Mr. Carlisle had one of his horses stolen the other night?" Emma asked as Clara admired baby Monroe.

"I didn't hear about that," Caroline said as she wrapped the last slice of cake.

"I saw Edie yesterday evening, and she mentioned overhearing Marshal Wright talking to Mr. Carlisle about it," Emma explained. They both looked to Clara for confirmation.

"It's true," she said quietly. "But I don't think he wants many people to know. It looks bad for the livery."

"We understand," Caroline said. She passed the wrapped slices of cake across the counter to Clara. "I wonder if it's someone Mr. Carlisle knows? Someone angry at him, perhaps, or jealous."

That hadn't occurred to Clara at all. She wondered if Roman had thought of it.

"It's likely just someone passing through, or a man in a hurry to leave town. Unfortunately, this town is no stranger to outlaws," Emma said.

"Oh?" Clara asked, her curiosity piqued.

"Oh, but it's a good town," Caroline said quickly, likely misinterpreting Clara's curiosity for fear.

"But we have many fascinating stories," Emma said, her face alight. "We both used to work in the hotel, before we married."

"I'd love to hear about that," Clara said, clutching her packages.

"Then perhaps we can all meet for tea one day," Caroline suggested.

"Perhaps Sunday, after you close the store?" Emma said.

The ladies agreed on a time, and Clara left, feeling light despite the growing clouds in the sky. Making friends made Crest Stone feel more like home, and it took away some of the sting of not being able to confide in Violet daily.

She delivered one slice of cake to Miss Darby, who was beside herself with joy at receiving the gift. With the other two packages, Clara made herself wait impatiently in the parlor.

What would Roman think about Caroline's idea that the thief was someone he knew? She hadn't told Roman this, but she secretly hoped that by working at the livery, she might overhear something useful. She knew Roman had written off the loss of his horse, but Clara still held hope that someone knew who the thief was. Even if the man was long gone, simply knowing his name would make it more difficult for him to ever return and take advantage of Roman again.

But even if she didn't hear a thing about the theft, she enjoyed greeting the livery's customers, answering their questions, and collecting payment for board and rent. And even better, Roman had seemed pleased with her efforts yesterday.

If she proved herself useful enough, maybe he'd overlook whatever it was that had driven Gideon away.

Chapter Nine

"DO YOU SUPPOSE THAT could be a possibility?" Clara finished after expounding upon a theory relayed to her by the mercantile owner's wife.

Roman was more dismayed that word about the theft had made it past the marshal, but he supposed it was inevitable in a town this small. At least Clara seemed confident in Mrs. Drexel's promise that she and Mrs. Hartley wouldn't discuss it with anyone else.

"I doubt that's the case," he said. He had no enemies in town—none that he knew of anyway. He'd gotten along with everyone since the day he'd arrived. He had no cause to think that any one of them would intend him harm. He'd certainly made an enemy or two in his past, particularly during his time at the Flying O Ranch, but that was two years ago, and several miles north of Cañon City.

"Well, it was worth a thought, although I'm glad to hear no one has any ill intentions toward you," Clara said with a smile.

A man stepped into the livery at just that moment, to inquire about renting a horse. Roman stepped back and let Clara take care of the transaction. She deftly handled the exchange of money with a smile and lighthearted conversation that soon had the man chuckling in response. Roman fetched the horse, and the man left with a grin on his face.

"How did I do?" Clara turned to Roman.

"I'd say you're a natural when it comes to people," he replied. "Although I am curious how you might do with horses."

"Horses love me," she said confidently. He believed her, especially considering how well she'd gotten on with Tartan yesterday. But he couldn't let the moment pass without a challenge.

He eyed her dress, a clean, pretty thing that wasn't as fancy as the blue one she'd worn yesterday, but was still hardly the stuff of a stablehand.

"I'm not afraid of a little dirt, if that has you concerned," she said, her hands on her hips and her chin lifted.

"All right, then. Follow me." He led her past the stalls to one of the rooms in the rear, where he grabbed a curry comb and a brush, before taking her outside to the corral. "Wait here," he instructed before handing her the tools.

She stood by the corral fence, under the gray clouds that moved quietly across the sky. Roman entered the corral, selected a gelding that belonged to Jeremiah, attached a halter and lead rope, and led the animal to a small enclosure just outside the corral. After securing the horse, he opened a gate to the enclosure and gestured at Clara to join him.

"This is Robin Hood," he said, stroking the bay's neck.

Clara smiled at the animal. "Steals from the rich to give to the poor?"

"Mostly just eats more than any other horse in the place. He's Jeremiah's." Roman tried not to grin too much when Clara lifted a hand and petted Robin Hood on the nose. Before she'd arrived, he'd feared she might be afraid of the horses. But nothing could be further from the truth. In fact, she didn't even complain about the smell of the livery, which caused most ladies to wrinkle their noses upon entering.

"Does he need a brushing?" Clara asked, holding up the brush and curry comb he'd given her earlier.

Roman scrutinized the horse's coat. He was dusty, as usual, but Jeremiah hadn't had a moment to groom him yet this morning. "This fellow loves a roll in the dirt, so he needs grooming more often than most. Want me to show you?"

She nodded and held out the brush and curry comb. He took the curry comb and began to work the dirt out of Robin Hood's coat in strong but gentle circles. Fine bits of dust flew off the horse's coat as he worked. Roman handed the comb back to Clara, who had removed her gloves.

She lifted it as he had and began to move it over the horse, very gently.

"You have to put more into it. Like this." Roman reached around her and laid his hand on top of hers. The warmth of her small hand under his instantly made it hard for him to remember what he was doing. His thoughts churned like wagon wheels through mud, and he had to force himself to think through the simple act of currying a horse.

"Like so," he said, his voice a shade lower than normal.

"I see," Clara said after a second.

He lifted the comb again and led her hand farther down the horse. Robin Hood stood patiently, which was why Roman had chosen him. As much as the gelding enjoyed getting dirty, he also took pleasure in getting cleaned up.

Clara shifted slightly in front of Roman, and he stepped forward to compensate for the movement. It brought him even closer to her, and he curled away as best he could even though every fiber in his body wanted to wrap itself around her and protect her from all the terrible things in the world.

Too late, he realized that he'd stopped moving the curry comb. Clara turned in front of him, her green-gray eyes catching his, and her hand still trapped beneath his own.

"Thank you for showing me," she said, her voice a whisper. She swallowed visibly.

The moment was too much, too soon. Roman forced himself to remove his hand from hers and step back.

Cool morning air flooded his lungs, and the sounds and scents of the corral and the town around them suddenly came back to life. What had just happened? It wasn't as if he'd never been close to a woman before, but he'd never felt anything quite like that. He needed to be alone, to think, to remember who and where he was.

He forced himself to breathe and then to smile. "I think you've got it. I'll be back in a moment."

With that, he escaped from the enclosure, and took a few steps toward the stable, before stopping and turning back. "Perhaps you'd like to have dinner tonight? With me?" he added, barely conscious of the words coming from his mouth.

She smiled at him, parting the clouds with her cheerful disposition. "I'd love to."

Roman nodded and walked into the stable, wondering just what exactly he'd gotten himself into.

Chapter Ten

CLARA TOOK HER TIME getting ready for dinner. After a day of brushing horses and assisting customers, her calico had collected far too much dust and dirt to be appropriate to wear to eat anywhere except in a barn.

She had only the blue dress she'd worn yesterday, and the soft green one she'd arrived in. That one had since been cleaned, thanks to her new friend Abigail at the boarding-house, and so she opted for it. It was her favorite, with the way the lighter green bodice and overskirt set off her eyes, and the darker green underskirt was the color of the forests back home in Virginia. She then unwound her hair, gave it a good brushing, and repinned it into a looser chignon with a few tendrils framing her face.

Altogether, she was pleased at her efforts, and she hoped Roman would take notice.

As she waited for him in the parlor, she thought back on what had happened between them earlier in the day. He'd made himself awfully scarce afterward. Although she wasn't certain why, she was almost glad to have the time to recompose herself. His hand had been warm and reassuring over hers, and his breath had warmed her neck as they worked. She'd been so consciously aware of how close he was that it was a wonder she hadn't collapsed into a heap right there on the ground. She'd had to put every effort into keeping the brush in her hand and remembering to breathe.

Whatever it was that had passed between them, it was nothing like she'd ever experienced with Gideon. When he'd taken her hand, all she could think about was how damp his palm was and how she'd wished she'd kept her gloves on. He was handsome enough, for certain, and he'd made her heart beat a little faster sometimes. She'd thought that was simply how it felt to be attracted to a man.

She'd been wrong. Very, very wrong.

The door opened, and there he stood, dressed in the gray suit Clara had met him in. A giggle rose from her throat, and she pressed a hand to her mouth. It did no use, however, and her laughter escaped around her fingers.

"What is it?" He looked alarmed, his hat in one hand and the other patting down his coat and vest.

"It's nothing . . ." Clara swallowed her giggles and gestured helplessly at the two of them. "Only that we both apparently used up our nicest clothing when we first met each other."

It took a moment, but he finally smiled. Clara breathed a sigh of relief. She'd been afraid for a second that he'd take her observation as an insult rather than a simple fact that neither of them seemed overly concerned with fanciful clothing.

"So it seems," he said. Then he extended an arm. "May I accompany you to dinner?"

"Please," she said, looping her arm through his.

When he opened the door, Clara paused. "Where are we going?"

Roman grinned. "I thought we might take our meal at the hotel restaurant."

Her eyes widened. "Are you certain?' She couldn't fathom how much that might cost.

"Absolutely."

Clara bit her lip as he led her down the road. A train idled on the tracks next to them. Was she dressed nicely enough? Surely folks coming off the train for a meal couldn't be bothered with wearing their finest clothing, and if they traveled with the windows open, they'd be covered in a fine layer of soot, as Clara knew all too well.

What might the hotel restaurant serve? She hoped it was food she could recognize. But she resolved to eat whatever they might set upon her plate. She wouldn't have Roman thinking he'd wasted his hard-earned money.

They strode up the hill to the imposing building as a carriage passed them, filled with people Clara supposed were heading back to board the train. At the top of the hill, he paused a moment by the hotel's fountain, allowing them both to look over the town spread out below.

"It looks so small from here," Clara said.

"It won't be long before it's spread out in all directions," Roman said, and Clara imagined he was right. With all the buildings and the people on the road below, she wondered how the town would look a year from now.

"Are you ready?" he asked.

When she nodded, he led them through the tall doors that formed the hotel's entry. Inside, Clara drew in a surprised breath. The ceiling soared above her, polished wooden beams holding it aloft. A staircase off to the right led to the second floor, which overlooked the large room in which they stood. The floor and walls were made of shining wood, and off to each side, a large stone fireplace kept watch over the sprawling space.

"I believe that's the dining room." Roman pointed to the left, where people of all sorts mingled. The sight of working men side by side with gentlemen and ladies put Clara's mind at ease. She need not have worried at all about her dress.

The dining room itself was just as impressive as the lobby, with white tablecloths and beautiful china place settings. They found an empty table near one of the windows.

Roman looked just as much in awe of the place as Clara was. "I must confess, I haven't been in this room before. I've taken a meal or two at the lunch counter, and if the food in here is half as good as it was there, I'm certain you'll enjoy it."

"I doubt I'd notice if it was simply cold chicken and a slice of stale bread," Clara said as she admired the napkins at each place setting that had been folded into flowers. "This entire room is a feast for the eyes."

Roman smiled, but before he could say another word, a young woman in a gray dress with a pristine white apron appeared beside them. She introduced herself as Miss Taylor, poured them some water, and took their orders.

An awkward silence settled over them after Miss Taylor left. Clara clasped her hands in her lap and let her eyes drift to the window, which had a view of the valley as it stretched toward the southeast. If she looked just so, she could make out the boardinghouse. "What must it be like to stay here and wake up to see this view in the morning?" she pondered aloud.

"Are you happy with the boardinghouse?" Roman asked.

Afraid he'd mistaken her musings for a complaint, Clara smiled at him. "Oh yes, I am. Miss Darby has become a friend, as have the two other ladies who are renting rooms. Thank you for . . ." She drifted off, uncertain how to phrase her gratitude for his payment of her lodgings.

"Of course. I could hardly have you sleeping in the stable. Jeremiah and I fit in well with the horses, but it's no place for a lady."

"I do enjoy helping, though."

Her words seemed to make him light up from the inside, his grin hiding the small scar above his lip. Clara smiled down at her hands, pleased she could make him so happy with just a few words.

"What made you want to start a livery business?" she asked, curiosity getting the better of her. All she knew from his letters were a few basic details about his family. Most of their written conversation had focused on his life here and personal traits.

Roman lifted his hands to the table and picked up a fork, examining the fine filigree that ran across the handle. "My father runs a stockyard back in Kansas City. I believe I wrote you about him."

Clara nodded.

"I grew up working with cattle—I was the only one of my brothers who enjoyed the work. They've all gone on to open less messy businesses," he said with a smile.

"How many brothers do you have?" She'd written to him of her four much younger siblings, but he hadn't elaborated much on his own.

"Three," he said quickly before moving on. "I didn't know what I wanted to make of my life for a long time. I worked my way across Kansas once I was grown, as a ranch hand and driving cattle to the rail lines. I kept moving west. I'm not sure why. Perhaps I thought I'd find whatever it was I was seeking if I kept moving on. Eventually I found myself working a ranch outside Cañon City, and then another one down here in the valley. I rode through here last fall, before this town was much of anything, and it seemed to come to me out of nowhere—that I ought to use my earnings to buy a couple of horses and start up a livery stable."

Clara listened, hardly able to believe the chance he'd taken. "What if someone else had arrived before you and started a livery?"

Roman shrugged. "Then I suppose I would've moved on to another place and tried there."

Clara gazed at him, trying to even fathom such bravery. Meanwhile, she would've resigned herself to a life of spinsterhood in Virginia if things didn't work out here with Roman.

Oh, how she wanted them to work out.

She dug her fingers into the fabric of her skirts, wishing the thought—and the pink that likely blossomed in her cheeks—would go away. "Your family must be very proud of you," she finally managed to say, just barely looking up at him.

He pressed his lips together. "Likely more skeptical than proud."

Clara wanted to know more. What sort of family wouldn't be filled with joy and pride that their son was running a thriving business in a growing town? She was trying to decide upon the best way to ask, when he spoke up first.

"How about your family?" He leaned forward. "What do they think about your travels?"

Clara swallowed her questions. "My dear friend Violet has been my greatest support. She wasn't convinced, not right away, but when she saw how determined I was, she helped me as best she could. She gave me some money, and she shared my excitement."

His eyes crinkled at that last line. "And your family?"

Clara rested her hands on the table, lest she permanently wrinkle her skirts. "My mother came around. She knew I wasn't happy after . . ." She let her words trail off, hoping Roman understood. She'd written to him of Gideon, in the briefest of terms. "My father wasn't so pleased with my decision. He accepted it, but he made it clear that he did not agree with it."

"I'm sorry you left on such poor terms with him." Roman reached across the table and rested a hand on one of hers.

The warmth of his touch gave her strength. Papa would come around if they married and she wrote to him of her happiness. He would never be satisfied that she was so far away, but she felt certain he'd be supportive of her once everything here was settled. And her younger sisters and brothers would be a comfort to him.

"For what it's worth, I am very happy you took the risk of coming here. For me." Roman's thumb brushed across the top of her hand, and the touch sent Clara's mind spinning.

Just at that moment, Miss Taylor arrived with their dinner. Roman pulled his hand away, and Clara tried to direct her thoughts to the food before them. As she chewed the tender potatoes and perfectly salted ham, she kept catching Roman's eyes from across the table.

And Clara decided that she, too, was very happy she took a risk on Roman.

Chapter Eleven

IT WAS NEARING MIDNIGHT when Roman returned Clara to the boardinghouse. She giggled at the scandal of it should Mr. or Miss Darby awaken to find her arriving back so late on Roman's arm, and Roman laughed too, thankful she found it amusing rather than appalling. Considering that they'd been strolling about the town after dinner, and checking in on Jeremiah occasionally at the livery, there was hardly anything scandalous about their time together, other than the late hour.

He'd taken her hand as they walked, and she'd blessed him with that smile. He forced himself to take a step back from her as they stood in front of the boardinghouse, lest he give in to the strong urge he had to rest his hands upon her face and kiss her.

"Might I escort you to church services in the morning?" he asked.

"I would love that," she said.

"At least the building is finished now. You ought to have seen it when it was partially built and Reverend Marsh insisted on holding services. More than one person had an unpleasant gift from a bird flying overhead. And then sometimes it would start to rain."

Clara giggled, pressing a hand over her mouth.

"Until the morning?"

She nodded, her smile lighting up the darkness. "Yes. Until morning. Good night, Roman."

He carried the thought of her sweet voice and bright face with him as he moved through the street back toward the livery. The Starlight was operating at capacity, evident through the framing that would eventually be its front wall. He'd opted to walk on the opposite side of the tracks from the saloon while he was escorting Clara earlier, but now he kept to the west, passing directly in front of the place.

Inside, Mitchell Turley was easy to spot, even amongst the crowd, as he shouted incomprehensible words to a song Roman didn't recognize. The man that had paid him to distract Jeremiah likely sat in this very saloon, just a couple of nights ago.

With a shake of his head, Roman stepped forward, away from the Starlight. It had been a one-time event, a misfortune. It was certainly something likely to happen again as the town grew, but Roman hoped he would have the resources to hire on more men before that became a problem. His customers had been happy with the services he provided. Not once had a man attempted to skip out of paying for board or to run off with a rented horse or wagon. Those who found themselves unable to pay had gladly agreed to work off their debts, and Roman had been thankful to have the short-term help.

No, it was nothing to worry too much about yet. His business was doing well, he was well on his way toward expanding, and he was finally doing something his family wouldn't look down on, provided he could make it successful. And he had Clara.

The thought of her alone made his steps lighter. She was all that he imagined she might be, and more. He couldn't have hoped to meet a better woman the traditional way—even if there were enough women in Crest Stone to accomplish such a feat. Once he married her, perhaps he'd finally measure up to his brothers in the eyes of their parents.

The livery was always slower on Sundays. Perhaps after services, and after treating Clara to lunch, of course, he could put in more time on the house. If he worked diligently, he could finish it by the end of the month. It would still need furniture and trimmings here and there, but it would be livable.

And that's when he could ask Clara to marry him.

Chapter Twelve

THE CHURCH SERVICE met Clara's every expectation. Reverend Marsh was an enthusiastic pastor, bringing the words of the Bible to life with his sermon, and the other people in attendance at the little church were friendly and welcoming. Clara was happy to recognize Caroline and Emma from the mercantile. Knowing those two ladies, along with Miss Darby and Abigail and Deirdre, who lived at the boardinghouse, Clara felt almost at home. Even the woman who had served them dinner at the hotel last evening, Miss Taylor, stopped to say hello.

And yet it was strange, too, to hear different sorts of birds through the open windows, singing along with the hymns, as she sat next to Roman. A distant hammering became the background to the service, from men who either didn't attend or who were in a rush to finish work.

All the while, Roman sat beside her, his pleasant baritone singing along with the hymns, and the secure warmth of his presence making her feel as if all was right with the world. Occasionally, they'd catch each other's eye and smile.

It was, Clara decided, the most enjoyable church service she'd ever attended.

"Would you like to have lunch?" Roman asked after they left the church.

Clara waved to Emma, with whom she planned to meet for tea later that afternoon at the mercantile. Emma was holding her baby and leaving at that moment with a tall dark-haired man Clara assumed must be her husband. Roman nodded to the man.

"I'd love to. I'm absolutely famished," Clara said. "I believe Miss Darby put on a roast back at the boardinghouse."

Roman offered his elbow, and Clara took it as they made their way down the road. "I have a much better idea. In fact, I might have already put it into motion with Miss Darby, so I hope you'll be agreeable to it."

"Oh?" Clara raised her eyebrows.

But Roman didn't answer. Instead, he rewarded her with a mysterious smile and escorted her to the boardinghouse. Once there, he left Clara in the parlor and disappeared through the dining room toward the kitchen. When he emerged with a closed basket and a jar of lemonade, she figured out at least one piece of the puzzle.

"Are we having a picnic?" She stood, delighted at the idea.

"Perhaps," was all Roman said, keeping up the mystery.

He led her behind the boardinghouse and past the hill where the hotel's stables sat near the building. Before long, they arrived at a line of trees. Roman wove between cottonwoods and pines, Clara just behind him. On the other side of the trees, they emerged alongside a quiet little stream.

"This is Silver Creek," Roman said, turning to see her reaction.

"It's . . . beautiful . . ." Clara trailed off, thinking the word wasn't quite enough for the scene that lay spread out before her. The creek was very low, but it still flowed silently along its way. Behind it, more trees sat watch as the ground began to rise in hills. And above the hills, the Sangre de Cristo Mountains towered, seemingly oblivious to the beauty they lent this tableau.

Roman set the basket down and tucked the jar of lemonade against a small stone before coming to join her. "Isn't it? I never saw anything like this as a boy. When I arrived in Colorado, I remember I stood looking at the mountains, aghast at their sheer size. But I still hadn't seen anything quite like this until I came to this valley. You ought to see the creek in May and June, when the snow is melting from the mountains. It resembles a small river then."

"I can't wait to see it." She pinched her lips together and tried not to look at Roman. She couldn't believe she'd just made the assumption—aloud—that she'd be here come next spring. Because the only way that would happen would be if he decided he wanted to marry her.

"Me too," he said.

Clara ventured a glance at him, trying to determine if he meant that he was looking forward to seeing it himself, or if he couldn't wait for her to see it.

But all he gave her was a quiet smile before gesturing at their lunch. "Would you care to eat?"

"I thought you'd never ask," she said.

Clara removed her gloves and opened the basket as Roman sat nearby, rather than on the other side. She ducked her head so he couldn't see the flush she felt creeping up her face. As she removed wrapped sandwiches, cold potatoes, and Miss Darby's wonderful berry cobbler from the basket, she felt as if she were overly conscious of every move she made.

Both she and Roman reached for the glasses at the bottom of the basket at the same time, his hand brushing against hers. They both laughed, Clara rather self-consciously, as she drew back to let him retrieve the glasses. She went to work opening the sandwiches as he filled their glasses with lemonade.

"I fear I ought to have brought something for us to sit upon," Roman said as he picked up a forkful of potatoes.

"Well, there don't seem to be as many bugs here as we had back in Virginia, at least." Clara examined her sandwich, which appeared to be sliced ham on buttered bread. "We'd be overrun with ants without a blanket or quilt."

"I can't say I've ever been on a picnic before," Roman replied.

Clara swallowed her bite of sandwich. "You haven't? Well, I suppose that now you can say you have."

"I doubt any picnic I might have had before this one would ever measure up."

Clara took another bite in the hopes it would keep her from smiling too much. When she finished chewing, she said, "I've been on a few. Mostly excursions with other ladies from church, or with a group of Violet's society friends. And once with . . ." She let the words disappear into the air, thinking she oughtn't talk about picnicking with Gideon.

"The fellow who broke off your engagement?" Roman supplied as he passed her the jar of potatoes.

Clara took it, grateful to having something to do with her hands. So Roman remembered that she'd written about Gideon. She nodded. "Gideon Maxwell." It felt strange to say his name aloud again. Despite it being under a week since her arrival here, she felt as if Virginia and her misfortune with Gideon were like something that had happened in a dream.

"He's the reason you went looking through the marriage advertisements." Roman spoke the words as a statement rather than a question, as if the fact didn't bother him one bit.

"Well, not entirely," Clara said as she speared a potato on her fork. "Some time had passed—he married—"

Roman raised his eyebrows disapprovingly, which made Clara happier than she cared to admit.

"I felt . . . restless, I suppose. None of the men who might have taken an interest in me particularly appealed to me. And I suppose I decided I wanted something different from the life my mother had." She paused and looked at Roman, who had already finished his ham and butter sandwich and who now leaned back on a hand as he listened to her.

"My family isn't well-off, but we aren't poor. We have a small home at the edge of the city, immediately adjacent to those around it. My father works hard each day, and my mother does the same at home. It isn't a terrible existence by any means, but when I stepped back and realized I would've had the same with Gideon—or with any other man who might have courted me—I felt so . . . so . . . disappointed."

It was funny to put it all into words now, when she couldn't have articulated her reasoning back when she chose to leave. It was true that she tired of seeing Gideon and his new wife each day, but that wasn't the entire reason she'd opted to write to Roman Carlisle. It was more like a convenient excuse that both she and those she loved could understand.

But now that she was here, she knew it was so much more than that.

Roman nodded as he mulled over his words. "I felt much the same when I left Kansas City. My brothers all did as they were expected—went to work in business, married, started a family. Each time I thought of living the same life as my father, it felt as if I couldn't breathe. I have all the respect in the world for him, but it wasn't the life I wanted."

"And now you find yourself starting a business and . . ." Clara's cheeks went warm as she let the sentence drift off.

Roman laughed as he stretched out his legs. "After nearly ten years of drifting and doing everything my father had warned me against."

"What changed?" It felt like such a forward sort of thing to ask, but Clara said it anyway. She wanted to know everything about him, and he certainly didn't look chagrined that she'd inquired.

Instead, he caught her gaze with those dark eyes as his expression grew more serious. "I grew tired of that life. Of the men I worked with, the constant moving about, the trail, the insecurity that came with throwing my pay away the moment I received it, the danger I always seemed to find. And I couldn't figure how I could be surrounded by so many people and yet feel so alone."

Clara swallowed. She'd felt the same in the last few months before she'd left Virginia—lonely, even when she wasn't alone. "Is the danger you mentioned how you found yourself with that scar?"

He ran a hand over his lip, where the small white mark cut into his skin. Clara wondered if that was the reason he kept himself clean-shaven. Surely it would stand out more if he wore a mustache.

"It is," he said, his gaze now on the creek as if his mind had wandered somewhere else.

Silence settled around them for a moment, the only sounds coming from the breeze through the trees and a few birds perched somewhere nearby. The trees blocked the constant hammering and building sounds from town, Clara realized, making it feel as if they'd traveled miles away.

She looked back at Roman, curiosity scratching at her mind. "What happened?"

"It isn't a tale for a lady," he said, his gaze finally drifting back to her.

Clara raised her eyebrows. "That only makes me want to hear it all the more. I'm certain I'll wholeheartedly dislike the man who caused you injury."

He smiled at her, the scar stretching into something unnoticeable. "That fellow you were to marry back in Virginia didn't know at all what he had."

The compliment warmed her, even though she still yearned to hear the story. "I don't know about that . . ."

"You do yourself a disservice, Miss Clara Brown." Roman stood suddenly and extended a hand down to help her up.

Clara delighted in the feel of her hand in his. He held on to it, even after she was standing. She ought to put the wrappings and glasses back into the picnic basket, yet the moment she looked down with that thought, Roman reached out and took her other hand, drawing her attention back up to him.

"I can finish the house by the end of the month. Granted, it will still need some work, and it'll have little in the way of furnishings, but it will be a solid place to live at least."

Clara searched his face, trying to discern what he meant. "That's good," she said. "It will be much more restful than sleeping in the livery, I'm certain."

A smile tugged at his lips. "I was hoping you might want to live there with me."

She drew her brows together. Was he asking . . . ?

"I'd like to marry you, Clara, if you'll agree. We would need to wait until the house is completed, of course . . ." He trailed off, looking at her intently. "Will you?"

Joy filled every part of her. After everything, her dreams were finally coming true. 'Yes. Yes, of course I will."

He grinned at her, her hands still in his, until he dropped them and instead, wrapped his arms around her. Clara buried her face into his chest, uncertain when she'd ever felt so content. He smelled of straw and tobacco, and if she could, she'd never leave this spot, safely held in his arms. How had she come to be so lucky? To take a chance as wild as this one and find a man like Roman?

Roman shifted, and Clara lifted her head to look up at him. His smile evened out as he gazed at her, and Clara's heart thumped harder. Was he to kiss her now? She wanted him to, so badly, and yet she feared she might lose all control of her senses if he did.

He lifted a hand and, ever so lightly, brushed his fingertips against her cheek. "Clara," he whispered.

Her eyes fluttered shut. And all she could think was that it was a good thing he still held on to her so firmly, else she'd lose the ability to hold herself upright.

Roman's breath was warm on her lips. She caught her breath, waiting—and then he was gone.

Chapter Thirteen

ROMAN HELD TIGHTLY to one of Clara's hands as he fought to focus on the voices he'd heard. Clara swayed just slightly next to him before following his gaze past the bend in the creek.

There, just beyond a few pines that jutted out, Roman spotted two people walking. Two ladies, in fact. They chattered as loudly as the birds in the trees. Roman straightened as they came into view, casting a quick glance at Clara, who appeared as dazed as a newborn foal. He bit down on his lip, trying not to think about how he was the one who'd had that effect on her.

"Good afternoon," one of the girls said as they came into full view.

Roman recognized the gray dresses and matching hats of the waitresses who worked in the hotel's restaurant. "Good afternoon, ladies," he said, his voice as clear as it could be considering he'd nearly ruined Clara's reputation.

He traced circles on the back of her hand with his thumb by way of apology. He ought to just let go completely, especially if he was so concerned with them remaining respectable. Just as the thought occurred to him, one of the girls noticed their entwined hands. Roman froze. It was too late. They'd be forced to announce their engagement immediately, else he'd risk not only Clara's reputation, but her safety.

But the girl grinned at them, happy, as if she was delighted to share in their secret.

Roman let out a breath as they walked past. Finally, he pulled his hand from Clara's. "I apologize. I shouldn't have taken such a liberty, particularly in so public a place."

But instead of looking upset, Clara merely smiled. "I believe my reputation is still intact, if that's what worries you." She bent down and expertly gathered the wrappings and glasses and placed them into the basket. "And besides," she said as she handed him the closed basket, "I rather enjoyed myself."

He stared at her a moment, and then burst into laughter. "I admit I enjoyed myself too. As far as picnics go, I doubt I'll ever attend another quite as perfect as this one."

"I should hope not," Clara said as she took the elbow offered. She wrapped her other hand around his arm as they walked, and Roman decided right then and there that he'd do anything for this woman.

He didn't know what it was about her—her innocent smile, her sharp wit, her forthright manner, the way she seemed to trust him implicitly—but he'd work his fingers to the bone to finish that house as soon as he possibly could.

And then he would marry her.

ROMAN PRESSED HIMSELF to finish his work in the livery as fast as possible that afternoon. Clara had retired to the boardinghouse to prepare for the tea she was to attend later that afternoon, and Roman knew she was looking forward to sharing their good news with Miss Darby and her friends. If he finished his work in the stable, he could likely persuade Jeremiah to attend to any customers and take care of feeding and stabling the horses for the night.

And that meant he could put in several hours' work on his house.

Their house.

Roman braced the stall door back into place and prepared to hammer the new bolt into the hinge. Pender, Monroe Hartley's horse, was a crafty thing. He'd managed to pull the bolts from the original hinges night after night, pushing the door open and wandering about the stable. Benton, the blacksmith, had created a new sort of hinge and bolt after Roman had explained the predicament. This one, Benton claimed, was horse-proof. Roman hoped the man was right.

"I've never seen you so happy about replacing a perfectly good hinge." Jeremiah leaned against the next stall.

"I'm not, particularly," Roman said. "Although you have to admire Benton's ingenuity in creating it." He looked at the new hinge and smiled, although his mind had already wandered back to Clara.

Jeremiah shook his head. "I suppose you and Miss Brown had a nice time together. Else you wouldn't be looking at that hinge as if it were made of gold."

Roman tried to look serious, but it was almost impossible. "We did."

"Customers sure do like her."

Roman felt the corners of his mouth turning up again. "She does lend a certain joy to the place, doesn't she?"

"You don't ask that girl to marry you soon, some other fellow will," Jeremiah said.

Roman turned a glare on him.

Jeremiah straightened and held up his hands. "Didn't say *I* would. Just saying it'd be a shame to let a sweet girl like that slip through your fingers."

"Hmm." He could tell Jeremiah he'd already asked her, and she'd already agreed, but it felt too soon. The light that sparked inside Roman each time he thought of it felt like something he wanted to keep for himself, just for today. His own private source of happiness. He could share the news tomorrow, before he went to fetch Clara.

"If you want to put some time in on the house, I can hold things down here for the evening," Jeremiah said, as if he'd read Roman's mind.

"I'd appreciate that." With one last swing of the hammer, the bolt was in place. Roman pushed the stall door open and closed to test it. "And that ought to keep Pender put for the night."

"We hope," Jeremiah said, his attention moving toward the front door. "Looks like Potter's back."

"You sure you don't need me?"

"I've got it. You get on to working on that house, so you can marry that girl already." Jeremiah winked at him and made his way toward the front of the stable.

Thoughts of Clara followed Roman to pick up some tools in the back room, and continued to follow him as he walked outside and around the corral. He absentmindedly scratched the nose of a paint pony that belonged to one of the men in town before striding back to the unfinished house. He stood inside, letting his eyes travel the length of the beams around him. There was a lot still to be done.

He retrieved wood from the lean-to and set to work, cutting and fitting, hammering and nailing. Images of Clara floating about the finished house, hanging pictures and setting dinner on the stove and reading in the parlor, kept him company while he worked. Jeremiah brought him a plate of slightly burnt beans and a slab of crusty bread just as the sun began to set. Roman retrieved a lamp and continued to work.

He didn't know the time when he stepped back to admire the two finished exterior walls. It actually looked like a house now, with spaces cut out for windows and a door. He smiled as the stars twinkled overhead, then walked inside the house to see how it all looked from there.

Inside, he raised the lantern to examine the walls. He'd done good work, particularly for someone who'd never built more than a fence before a few months ago. He sat back against one of the walls in the parlor, setting the lantern beside him. The room would be big enough to hold a settee and perhaps a chair or two in front of the fireplace, but small enough to be cozy on a cold winter's night.

Roman looked up at the stars shining between the beams of the ceiling. He could just make out the frame of the second-floor room that sat above the bedroom.

A home of his own. He couldn't even have imagined such a thing a few years ago. When it was complete, he'd pay a photographer to come down from Cañon City and take an image of himself and Clara in front of the house to send home to his parents. It may not be one of the fine city homes his brothers lived in, but he'd have built the place with his own hands.

It was surely something they could be proud of.

He ought to put the tools up and take himself to bed. Morning couldn't be all that far off. But the view here was so nice, and it wasn't all that uncomfortable . . .

Roman's eyes drifted closed as he imagined Clara's smile upon seeing the house again.

Chapter Fourteen

"JUST THINK, YOU MIGHT be the first to be married in the church here!" Abigail Regis said, her jam and bread forgotten on her plate.

"Oh no, I believe someone was married there in June, before it was even complete," Deirdre Hannan said. She'd come to Crest Stone a few months ago with her brother, who was helping to build many of the businesses and homes in town. "A rancher and his wife, if I remember correctly. It was before you arrived, Abigail. And then the marshal and Edie were married there too."

Clara smiled, her breakfast already finished, as her two new friends and fellow boardinghouse residents discussed her wedding. She was famished this morning, having already polished off four thick slices of Miss Darby's bread and preserves.

"We've only just become engaged. We haven't yet even discussed a wedding," she said.

"Oh, but it's just so wonderful to think about, isn't it?" Abigail asked, clasping her hands together. She had come to town to find housekeeping work, but with there being none available, she'd decided to start taking in laundry.

"It is," Clara admitted.

"And *when* you're ready, we'll help with anything you need," Deirdre said with a smile.

"That would be wonderful." Clara bit her lip as she looked down at her empty plate. It was so strange to be talking about a wedding without her mother or Violet. How many times had Mama reminisced over her own simple wedding? And Violet and Clara had been dreaming of their own special days since they were girls.

But she was happy to have made new friends, such as Deirdre and Abigail, and Emma and Caroline. She couldn't wait to stop by the mercantile later on to share her news with Caroline. And then perhaps she could visit Emma's home and tell her.

There were still two hours remaining before Roman would come to escort her to the livery. But Clara was far too restless to wait, and besides, it felt as if it had been days since she'd last seen him, never mind that it had only been since yesterday. Fetching her hat from her room, she decided she would arrive early and save Roman the time away from his work. It was so very thoughtful of him to come get her each day, but it was entirely unnecessary, especially now that she was more familiar with the town. It was difficult for one to become lost when a town consisted of only one street.

Clara adjusted the ribbon under her chin and smiled at herself in the little mirror that sat perched on the washstand. Something about being so happy made her face light up. She'd never considered herself particularly pretty, but looking at her reflection now, she believed she could see what it was that Roman saw.

In fact, everything about the day felt bright and cheer-ful—the polished handrail along the boardinghouse stairs, the blue sky, the morning chill in the air, the half-finished build-ings along the road, even the saloon, which she generally thought of as somewhat menacing. Now, a questionable sort of fellow who stood outside nodded a greeting at her, and Clara smiled and inclined her head in return.

The early sun shone onto the livery. The front doors were opened, ready for business. Clara picked her way across the road and the tracks, and paused at the entrance.

Just inside stood a man in a long coat, talking with Roman and Mr. Wiley. Their faces were drawn and serious. Clara slid quietly through the doorway and stood aside, waiting for them to finish. Roman glanced her way, his eyes lingering on her for a just a fraction of a second before returning to the man before him. Mr. Wiley gave her a slight smile, which she returned.

"A night watch is a good idea," the gentleman in the coat was saying. "Meanwhile, I'll keep my ears open." He turned, and Clara caught sight of the metal badge pinned to the vest under his coat.

He must be the town marshal. She swallowed, fear edging out the cheer she'd woken with. Something must have hap-pened, else he wouldn't be here. Roman had mentioned that Marshal Wright and his wife currently lived in the hotel, and as such, he kept his horse in the hotel stables and not at Ro-man's livery. And then there was the dark look on Roman's face, a barely contained facade concealing what could be a hun-dred different emotions. Even Mr. Wiley's usual lightearted-ness was gone, replaced by something more troubled.

"I appreciate that, Marshal," Roman said, shaking the man's hand.

"Let me know if you need assistance. I can round up a few trustworthy men to help you watch the place, if need be," the marshal said as the group moved toward the door. "Miss," he said, with a tug of his hat when he spotted Clara.

"Good morning, Marshal," she forced herself to say, when what she really wanted was to demand to know why he was here. Was it the horse thief? Had he returned?

The men parted ways, the marshal headed back into town, while Mr. Wiley fairly ran off to the rear of the building. Only Clara and Roman stood up front, the cool breeze lifting bits of straw from the floor and sending them scuttling across the dirt.

Roman stood silently, fixing that angry gaze out into the street, his hands on his hips, even as a bird sang nearby and the smithy greeted someone with a loud, friendly shout next door.

Clara paused, uncertain what to do. She wanted desperately to know what had happened, to help in some way, and yet, she had the distinct feeling that Roman might need to be left alone with his thoughts. So she opted to remain in place, quiet and waiting for whenever he needed her.

A few minutes later, he finally turned and seemed to notice her presence. "Clara," he said, drawing out his pocket watch. After checking the time, he looked back up at her. "I was coming to get you closer to ten."

"I awoke early and hadn't much to keep me occupied at the Darbys' and . . . I wanted to see you." Clara took a step forward.

Roman returned the watch to his pocket and glanced out to the road beyond the door. "It isn't safe for you to wander about town alone."

Clara thought back to her walk from the boardinghouse. Nothing about it had felt unsafe. Not even the saloon.

Roman continued to stand at the door, his attention focused on whatever—or whomever—was outside. Clara quietly joined him, but when she glanced out, she saw nothing beyond the dirt road, the railroad tracks, and the buildings in various states of construction on the other side. One man stood in front of one of those buildings, watching and waiting for something on down the road.

Clara glanced up at Roman, who still looked at nothing outside. "Roman?" she said quietly. "What happened?"

He drew in a deep breath, expelling it before speaking. "Someone stole two horses last night."

"That's terrible. I'm sorry." It felt like such a trivial thing to say, entirely unhelpful, but it was all Clara could come up with. She laid a hand on his arm.

Roman continued to let his gaze travel up and down the road outside, as if he were searching for something.

"Which horses were taken?" she finally asked. Although she'd only been helping at the livery for a short while, there were a few horses she'd come to know better than others. She hoped it wasn't Tartan, the banker's horse, or sweet Georgia, who was one of Roman's own.

"Baxter and Felicity. Boarded horses," Roman said, his mind clearly elsewhere.

Clara's heart sank. It was bad enough to have one of his own horses stolen, but now to have others under his care go missing too? Clara wanted to pull him close to her and tell him all would be well, but he stood like a stone, unmoving and preoccupied. And so she remained where she was, one hand gently placed on his arm, in case he needed her.

She said nothing for a moment, trying to imagine how the men who owned those horses might react. "Do they know yet? The men who boarded the horses."

Roman made a sound that indicated they didn't, and Clara said a quick prayer that the men would be understanding. That they wouldn't blame Roman.

She wanted to know how it happened, when it happened, every detail. But it wasn't the right time to ask Roman such things. And so she kept her questions to herself until Mr. Wiley appeared up front an hour later to take a new customer's horse. Clara was grateful Roman and Mr. Wiley *had* new customers. Once the men who owned the missing horses learned what had happened, she feared others might not trust the livery to keep their animals safe.

With the customer gone and the new horse turned out in the corral, Clara could contain her curiosity no longer. She hadn't seen Roman since he'd finally left his watch at the door to assist his customer, but Mr. Wiley had come back up front and went to work cleaning out a stall nearby.

And so Clara left her post at the desk and walked the few steps over toward where Mr. Wiley tossed out a clump of dirty straw.

"Miss Brown," he said, pausing in his work. His usual smile was there, but strained, and Clara knew what had happened weighed heavily on him. "I hope your morning has gone well."

"It has, thank you," she replied, resting her hands on the top of the open stall door. She glanced back into the stable to ensure Roman wasn't nearby. "Roman is quite worried about what happened last night."

Mr. Wiley removed his hat and tapped it against his thigh. Dust flew off the brim. "And rightly so." He replaced the hat.

"May I ask you what happened? Roman isn't . . . well . . ." She trailed off, uncertain what else to say.

Mr. Wiley nodded in understanding before replacing his hat. "We don't know much. I was asleep in the back room. Roman fell asleep in the house out behind the corral—he was working late out there. We both awoke about sun-up and found the two horses closest to the front up here gone."

Clara furrowed her brow. The thief certainly knew how to execute his crime quietly enough so as not to wake Mr. Wiley. Perhaps that's why the man took only horses from the front of the stable. "How did he get inside?"

Mr. Wiley shrugged. "Walked in, I suppose. We can't lock the place up in case there's a fire."

"Yes, that makes sense," Clara said.

"We've been too trusting. Thought that one theft was all that would happen. We should've set up a watch after that." He ran a hand over his short, somewhat unkempt beard. "Mighty sure Roman's blaming himself for not doing so."

"He couldn't have known it would happen again. Do you suppose it's the same person?"

"Wouldn't know. Possible, I suppose."

Clara chewed her lip as she thought. "If it was the same person, he might've thought you did have a watch set up, given that he had to distract you from the door the first time."

"Well, we must've made his night this time around, then." Mr. Wiley glanced into the stall he'd been cleaning. "We're going to have to hire on more men. Roman and I can't work all day then stay up half the night. Don't know how we're going to do that, though . . ."

Clara's heart ached for Roman and Mr. Wiley. They'd been in business such a short while. It wasn't right that they had to face such a terrible problem.

"Hello?" A gentleman stood near the front door, his eyes searching the dim light of the stable.

"Good morning," Clara said brightly as she left Mr. Wiley to greet the customer.

The man was young and nicely dressed. As usual when she met someone new at the stable, Clara was instantly curious about who the man was and what he did. He must be in business of some sort, she thought, given how he was dressed. "What can we do for you today?"

"I need to take my horse out for the day. Felicity." The gentleman smiled at her, completely unaware his was one of the horses that had been stolen.

Uncertain what to say, Clara glanced to Mr. Wiley, who'd overheard the conversation. He brushed off his gloved hands and left the stall.

"Ought I fetch Roman?" she asked quietly after he greeted the customer.

Mr. Wiley nodded, and Clara left as quickly as possible. She didn't want to see the poor man's reaction when Mr. Wiley told him what had happened.

She found Roman out back, between the stable and the corral. He'd set out several pieces of wood next to the start of the wagon he'd been working on, yet he wasn't working. Instead, he stood, a couple of nails in his hand, staring at the wood on the ground.

Clara shivered and wrapped her arms around herself. Summer here was different than it had been in Virginia. There, the temperatures would be pleasantly warm by this time in the morning, and headed well toward uncomfortably hot in the afternoon with a dampness in the air that made it difficult not to perspire just sitting still. Here, she needed a coat or a shawl before midday.

"Roman?" she said hesitantly, not wanting to interrupt his thoughts.

He looked toward her and seemed to come back to life. For just a second, she saw him as he'd been yesterday—a smile and a light in his eyes that let her know he was glad to see her. Then it disappeared, as if it had never been there. The frown returned, worry etching lines into his face, and his eyes darkened.

"The gentleman who boards Felicity is here. Mr. Wiley is speaking with him."

"Thank you," he said shortly, dropping the nails into the wooden crate on the ground that held his tools. Without a look backward, he disappeared through the doorway.

Clara stayed put, hugging herself even more tightly as unease crept through her. If she didn't know better, she'd have thought Roman was angry with her.

He is preoccupied with worry, she told herself. That was all. She could hardly expect smiles and affection when such a terrible thing had just happened to his business. And especially when he had to face down a potentially angry customer.

He was not Gideon. He cared for her and wanted to marry her, and she felt the same about him. Clara looked out over the corral filled with horses. This place was so important to him, which meant that it was important to her too. She would do all she could to help him with his work.

Chapter Fifteen

THE DAY DIDN'T IMPROVE as the morning stretched on.

Jeremiah had already explained to Frederick Templeton what had happened with his horse by the time Roman arrived. The man was upset, of course, and Roman gave him more than what old Felicity was worth. The man didn't ask for it, but Roman almost felt obligated to do so. Those horses were under his care, and now they were gone. Then he decided to get the other meeting he was dreading done with, and so he took most of what he had left and found Yancy Wise, a man who'd only been in town for about a week. Wise was harder to deal with than Templeton, but finally agreed to take the money.

If anything else happened before he could collect enough in boarding and rental fees, Roman would be selling off one of his own two remaining horses to survive.

Now he stood just inside the stable door, staring again out into the road. He didn't know what he was looking for. An unfamiliar face, perhaps, but there were plenty of those in Crest Stone lately. It was pointless, he knew even as he stood there. The man—or men—who'd taken horses from him twice were likely long gone.

Were they the same person, or was it just bad luck? Why were they stealing his horses and none from the hotel livery?

He'd stopped by and visited Frank Robbins up there after paying Yancy Wise to let them know to be on guard. They'd had no trouble at all. Was it because he was on the edge of town and they were safe up on that hill?

Why hadn't he insisted on keeping watch after the first time? It wasn't a mistake he'd make again. Jeremiah had already volunteered to take first watch, but Roman knew they couldn't go on like that for too long. He needed to hire on more men for that purpose. But with what money? And how could he know who to trust? Marshal Wright had offered to help find men, but he wouldn't have known them any longer than Roman did..

A rustling sound from behind him drew his attention away from the worries that seemed to parade down the dirt road. Clara stood by the desk, which was only a few slabs of wood nailed together, where they kept the ledger and a running list of clients and horses. The formerly dusty desk was clean, he noticed. And polished to a shine, with the ledger and client books stacked neatly and two pencils, the pen, and the inkwell and blotter arranged in a perfect row. It must have been Clara's doing.

She watched him now, her eyes green in the sunlight that filtered through the open doors. It felt as if he were seeing her for the first time all day, although he knew she'd been here the entire time.

Here, in his stable, where in the dead of night, a thief made off with two horses. Again. He had no idea who the man was, or what he was capable of. For all he knew, the fellow had already sold off the horses in the mining encampment or to some rancher who didn't ask questions and was headed back to Crest

Stone now. Or there may be multiple men. They might be lurking outside of town, just waiting for the opportunity to return.

This wasn't a place where any lady should be. Particularly if both he and Jeremiah were off working outside or somewhere in the back, leaving her up here all alone. He had enough on his mind that he couldn't worry for Clara's safety on top of all of that.

"Did you wear a coat?" he asked her.

"A shawl." She gestured at a piece of clothing folded neatly and lying over the back of the chair at the table.

He picked it up and laid it over his arm. "I'll walk you back."

"But it's only two o'clock." Clara tilted her head in confusion.

"It would be selfish of me to keep you here. It's far too dangerous." He led the way to the door, and finally, she stepped forward and joined him.

"I doubt it's—"

He held up a hand. "Please, Clara. I can't watch over you all day."

She bristled. "You certainly needn't watch over me. I'm perfectly capable of doing that myself."

"That isn't what I meant." Roman closed his eyes and pinched the bridge of his nose between his thumb and forefinger. He was losing horses—and likely customers—left and right. There were horse thieves on the loose. And now he'd gone and angered the woman with whom he'd hoped to spend his life.

He exhaled as he opened his eyes. "All I meant is that I can't worry for your safety while Jeremiah and I are occupied elsewhere. And if anything happened to you, I . . . " He'd never forgive himself.

Clara pressed her lips together, seemingly considering what he'd said. He extended a hand. Finally, she took it and let him lead her back to the boardinghouse.

They didn't speak as they walked, and he feared she was still angry with him. Well, if she was, then so be it. He'd rather her be mad than hurt, or worse, dead.

When they reached the door to the boardinghouse, she extended her hand for the doorknob, but he held her back. Clara turned, frowning just slightly. Roman didn't know how anyone could look so beautiful while being angry, and yet Clara did. Her skin was luminous in the afternoon light, and her eyes seemed a bright green. He wanted to press his lips to her turned-down ones, make them smile again. Yet he had the distinct feeling she'd slap him if he did such a thing right now.

"You can't be angry with me for wanting to protect you," he finally said.

The frown remained in place, but her face softened some. "I suppose," she said after a moment.

She still seemed hesitant, but this wasn't something he would change his mind about. So instead, he placed his hands on her cheeks. Her skin went pink beneath his touch and her eyes widened.

"Roman, you can't— Not here—"

He smiled, for the first time that entire day, and dropped a kiss on her forehead before letting her go. She was still flushed when he opened the door for her and ushered her inside.

Something about Clara made everything seem a little brighter. But as he stepped away from the boardinghouse and faced the town, the worry returned. And this time, it wasn't just about the fate of his business or how little money he had left.

How could he provide for Clara if it all fell apart?

Doubts pushed in from all sides, and Roman clenched his fists, forcing the thoughts away. He and Jeremiah would take turns keeping watch at night. As soon as he had enough money in his pockets again, he'd see about hiring a man or two to help out.

There would be no more stolen horses. Not while he had breath left in his body.

Chapter Sixteen

SIX DAYS HAD PASSED, and all Clara had seen of Roman was a brief moment here and there, when he'd either stop by the boardinghouse or, on one occasion, when she prevailed upon Miss Darby for the supper leftovers and brought them wrapped up to the livery. She missed helping at the stables, missed meeting the people who'd come to get a horse or pay their boarding fees, but most of all, she missed Roman.

How could she feel so strongly about someone she'd known for less than two weeks? She'd known Gideon for years, and while she'd been heartbroken at his rejection, she now knew she'd never felt as tied to him as she did to Roman.

Clara tried to fill her time, writing letters to Violet and her family, visiting with Emma and Caroline for tea, talking with Abigail and Deirdre, and helping Miss Darby with work around the boardinghouse. This morning, she'd gone to church, but Roman hadn't been in attendance. Keeping busy distracted her some from just how much she missed Roman. The quick visits helped, but even as she knew he tried to be attentive, it was easy to tell his mind was elsewhere. And try as she might, it was almost impossible to keep the worry from her mind when she went to sleep at night.

It was far too easy to imagine his attention drifting. To see him finding whatever fault Gideon had seen in her before he'd cast her aside. To imagine exactly how he might be changing his mind about her. When the sun rose, it banished the fear to some dark place deep inside. But it was always there, just waiting for a delayed visit or a lull in the conversation to send her spiraling into a night of fitful, unhappy dreams.

As the days passed, Clara thought on her promise to herself that she would help him as best she could. While she could hardly fight off a horse thief or sit up with a rifle to guard the livery at night, she might be useful in some other way.

If it had happened twice, it might happen again. She knew Roman feared the word getting around town, which it most certainly had after this last time. Perhaps Clara might help by simply listening. Someone, somewhere, had to know something. The man—or men—behind the stolen horses might have spent some time in town. And if they had, they likely would have made friends, or at least made themselves known at the various businesses about town.

With that in mind, Clara paid a visit to Caroline at the mercantile, who hadn't overheard anything, but who promised to keep her ears open. Clara highly doubted that horse thieves spent much time at fancy hotels, so she opted not to make the trek up the hill to find one of the familiar faces of the waitresses she'd seen about town. She spoke with the young boy who helped out at the depot, the smithy, and everyone else she'd met who might have the opportunity to overhear something of use.

Her tasks completed and not yet willing to return to the boardinghouse, Clara opted to follow the path she'd taken with

Roman for their picnic. Maybe the fresh air and quiet by the creek would help her think of other ways she might be helpful.

The sun had lowered itself behind the mountains by the time she emerged from the trees to the shallow, burbling creek, reminding her that she'd promised to help Miss Darby serve supper tonight. She didn't have long for her walk, and so she moved quickly, taking in the scenery as she went.

This truly was a beautiful place. The mere sight of towering peaks over the green of the aspens and pines and the sparkling blue of the creek made her breath catch in her throat. How could men such as the ones who'd stolen from the livery live in such a perfect place?

And what else could she do to help?

Thoughts wove through her mind, none of them particularly useful. Clara paused to watch a butterfly resting on a pretty yellow wildflower. She didn't know the names of any of the flowers that grew here. Perhaps that was something she could learn.

She was about to take a step forward, around a couple of large pines that jutted out from the line of trees that traveled the creek, when the sound of a voice made her pause. A male voice.

Clara's heart began to beat faster. She walked about town by herself, so often that it hadn't occurred to her that perhaps she oughtn't come down here by the creek alone. Not to mention that the only people she'd seen here with Roman were two friendly women. What sort of man was on the other side of those pines?

She swallowed hard and stood perfectly still. A second male voice answered the first, his words lost in the pounding of her heart in her ears. They seemed to be having a conversation between themselves. They couldn't have seen her behind these trees. If she turned and quietly walked away, they'd never know she was there.

So long as they stayed where they were and weren't strolling along the creek bank.

Clara forced herself to breathe more slowly, and just as she was about to turn to leave, her nose caught the scent of a cook-fire. Were the men sleeping here, by the creek? All the more reason she should leave now. Who knew what sort of men they were?

Yet as she turned again, she caught the actual words of their conversation.

" . . . Should've got more for that one. Gates is a cheat."

"You got someone better?"

"What about that fellow we met at Murray's?"

"The German? Nah, don't trust him."

"All I'm saying is he might buy at a better price."

"Ain't going to sell something half the county is looking for to someone I don't trust."

The other man grumbled something unintelligible.

Clara covered her mouth as their words sunk in. It could be nothing at all, but "something half the county is looking for" could certainly mean stolen goods.

Such as a horse.

Had she stumbled upon the thieves?

It couldn't be. It was far too simple. They could be talking about something else entirely, and yet . . . It made too much sense.

She had to get out of there and tell Roman. If they were back, it was for one reason: to take more horses. Silently, she turned as the men resumed their conversation, this time about the food on their fire. Everything in her screamed at her to run, but Clara forced herself to step slowly and cautiously. They didn't know she was there, and if she could remain quiet as she left, they'd be none the wiser.

The sun had slipped even lower in the sky, casting the creek in shadows. Clara watched the ground carefully as she walked to avoid stepping on branches or anything else that might make a sound. The call of an owl in a tree nearby startled her, causing her to stumble and step sideways, right onto a sizable branch.

The snapping sound it made as her foot struck and broke it in half seemed to echo along the creek.

The men beyond the trees went silent. She had to do something—*now*.

Without a second thought, Clara flung herself into the tree line and ran as fast as she could, heedless of any noise she was making. She didn't dare look behind her for fear it would slow her down. She kept running, and then, only when she'd crested the tree line and emerged far from the bottom of the hill where the hotel sat—and far from the edge of town itself—did she glance behind her.

No one was there, but that didn't mean they weren't somewhere back in the trees. She strained to listen, and sure enough, heard something moving through the leaves and bushes. The valley was flat here, with the boardinghouse in sight. If only she could make it there before they emerged from the trees.

But she knew that was impossible. It was too far, and the trees that sat by the creek weren't all that dense.

She had exactly one idea that might save her.

Clara stopped suddenly and turned. Breathing heavily, she patted down her skirts and walked calmly toward the south—as if she were simply a lady out for a sunset stroll from town. Her gaze flitted to the west, where the trees stood sentinel under the mountains. No one was in sight. Perhaps they were searching through the cottonwoods and pines instead. Or perhaps she'd imagined them behind her the entire time.

And then, just as she averted her eyes back toward the south, where the railroad tracks disappeared in the distance on their way to Santa Fe, she caught movement near the tree line out of the corner of her eye.

Ever so slightly, not turning her head, Clara looked toward the movement.

A man stood there, looking about. He spotted her immediately. It would look far too suspicious if she ignored him. A woman from town out for a little walk would certainly take notice of a man who suddenly appeared from behind the trees.

Drawing in a deep breath, Clara turned and looked directly at the man just as a second man joined him. All she could tell from this distance was that one wore a red shirt, and the other was dressed in shades of brown. They watched her for a moment. She inclined her head, even though she doubted they could see it from this distance.

She forced herself to look away and walk for another minute to the south, before turning and heading back toward town at a leisurely pace. When she glanced again toward the trees, the men were gone.

Her shoulders relaxed as she let out a breath. It had worked. Then she picked up her pace.

It was time to talk to Roman.

Chapter Seventeen

ROMAN PEERED AT THE names and numbers in the ledger books at the desk. Exhaustion from staying up half the night was starting to take its toll. He turned up the wick on the lamp for more light, hoping that it would also reveal more money to come in soon. If the banker paid tomorrow and he rented out both Georgia and the wagon, he might be able to breathe just a bit easier. It still wasn't enough to hire on anyone else—not after he'd had to repay Templeton and Wise for their stolen horses. But maybe after . . . Roman began adding up the numbers. After Friday next, if everyone—

"Roman!" a familiar female voice shouted from the one door that remained open.

He jerked his head up. Clara stood there, just inside the door. It was dark, far past any safe time for her to be outside alone. Roman jumped up.

"Clara, what are you doing here?" When he reached her, his gaze traveled her length. Her hair had escaped from its pins, her face was flushed, and her breath came quickly, almost as if she'd run here from the boardinghouse. He took her trembling hands in his. "What happened?"

"Oh, Roman, I believe I found them! The men who stole your horses."

That was the last thing he'd expected her to say. "How . . . ?" It was so improbable—so *impossible*—he couldn't even think of what to ask.

She told him of walking along the creek, alone. Roman bit his tongue at that revelation. And about how she'd stumbled upon a couple of men cooking their dinner while discussing the sale of something that most certainly sounded stolen. And if that weren't enough, about how she'd drawn their attention as she tried to leave and found herself running from them.

"Did they see you?" Ice crept through Roman's veins. Such men were often desperate. Whether they were desperate enough to worry about a woman having seen them . . . The very thought made Roman feel ill.

"Well . . . Not by the river. But I couldn't outrun them, so once I grew closer to the railroad tracks, I simply pretended I was a woman from town, out for an evening stroll."

He blinked at her. If the situation weren't so dire, he might have laughed. What other woman would have thought to do such a thing? "Did they believe the farce?"

"I think so. They certainly saw me, and I was far enough from town that if they thought I'd overheard them, well . . ."

Roman closed his eyes. He didn't want to imagine what might have happened.

"But instead they returned to their camp." Clara looked up at him with frightened eyes. "Do you suppose they've come back to steal from you again?"

Roman pressed his lips together. He didn't want to believe it. In fact, he didn't want to believe *any* of it. "Perhaps they were discussing something altogether different."

"Have you heard of anyone else in town having items stolen?" she asked, her eyes widening.

"No, but I doubt the marshal makes public every crime that occurs." No one wanted it known their business was easily robbed—Roman knew that firsthand. "It's possible they're just traveling through, on their way elsewhere."

"Yes," Clara said, but her voice didn't sound convinced.

"Jeremiah and I are staying up through the night, keeping guard," he replied, hoping that might assuage her fears.

"I know, but don't you think we ought to alert the marshal?" Her green-gray eyes looked to him for reassurance.

"I'll stop by the hotel and see him after I get you back to the boardinghouse." Roman returned to the desk for his hat and extinguished the lamp.

"Don't you think I ought to come too?"

"If he needs you, he can find you tomorrow at a decent hour." Roman took her elbow and led her to the door before turning to call back into the stable. "Jeremiah! I'm going out."

"All right, Boss," came the reply from somewhere in back. A horse shuffled in response, and Roman shut the door firmly behind him.

Roman led Clara down the road, his hand tucked protectively around her elbow. "You oughtn't be walking down by the creek—or anywhere outside of town—on your own."

"It was still daylight. I wouldn't do such a thing at night," she said.

He could feel her defiant eyes on him, and he sighed. He liked that about Clara, her spirit and her independent thinking, but not when it put her in danger. "I don't mean only at night."

"Are you telling me I can't stroll by the creek or out along the tracks or—or—anywhere when the sun is out?" Her voice matched the indignant look she was giving him.

"That is exactly what I'm saying. At least until we know the thieves are gone for good. If you need to walk, do so in town. Away from the saloon," he added.

"But—"

"Those men know who you are. Even if they believed your ruse this time, they certainly won't if they find you walking anywhere near their camp again." He looked down at her, hoping his words and the look he gave her firmly planted the danger she might face in her mind.

She said nothing. Instead, she pressed her lips together and turned forward, away from him.

"You shouldn't be walking alone anyhow, even in town, given what's been happening. I'd prefer if you took a companion."

She looked at him then, her eyes blazing brighter than the moon overhead. "I may not come assist you in the livery. I may not take a walk outside town. And now I must have a companion? Do you have any more rules you'd like to enforce, sir?"

Irritation shot through Roman. This was for her own good. Why couldn't she see that? "I only want to keep you safe."

"Do you suppose me entirely inept at doing that myself?" Her words cut into him.

"That is not what I said." He gritted his teeth together to keep from letting his annoyance form words he'd regret. "What sort of man would I be if I didn't protect you?"

She didn't answer. Instead, she sighed loudly, as if the very sensible things he'd asked her to do or to avoid were a heavy burden she had to bear.

Clara said nothing else as they walked, and he hoped that meant she accepted what he'd told her. His mind wandered to the men she'd encountered. Could it be they were the thieves? If so, it didn't bode well that they'd returned. In fact, that could only mean one thing.

They intended to steal from him again.

At least he and Jeremiah would be ready for them this time.

He bade Clara good night at the boardinghouse door. She wasn't happy with him, not in the least. That much was evident from the set of her jaw and the way she regarded him. He didn't dare try to take her hand or place a kiss on her cheek. It was better to let the anger simmer out of her. Once she calmed down, she would understand he only had her best intentions at heart.

As he stepped away from the Darbys' boardinghouse, he pushed away that aggravating voice in his head, the one that told him he wasn't enough to either provide for her or keep her safe. The same voice that insisted his livery would fail. That he wasn't good enough to be this kind of man, the one who ran a business and had a family.

Roman shoved those thoughts far down as he climbed the dark hill to the hotel. He already had too much on his mind to pay any attention to old fears. At the hotel, he alerted the marshal about the men camping by the creek and what Clara had overheard. The man agreed it was questionable what the strangers meant, but promised to pay them a visit at first light. Roman reassured him that he and Jeremiah had the livery covered for tonight.

He strode back down the hill as the shouting and music streamed out of the Starlight past the other side of the depot. Music? Roman paused a moment, listening. Sure enough, a piano banged out a raucous melody. He didn't remember the place having music before. They must've gotten that piano delivered on the train from Cañon City today.

A good whiskey would soothe some of the anxiety that seemed to never fully disappear these days, but Roman pressed on. He knew firsthand that spirits never cured a thing except a purse that was too full of coin, and besides, he needed a clear head at night if he had any hope of keeping his business going.

He pushed the front door open when he returned to the livery. It was as dark as he'd left it. Roman retrieved the lamp from the desk, lighting it carefully. He held it aloft. There was no sign of Jeremiah.

The horses were all in for the night, fed and watered. Jeremiah must be in the back room. Roman had agreed to take first watch, and the man was probably eagerly awaiting his return so he could get some much-needed rest.

"Jeremiah, I'm back," Roman called out as he walked between the two rows of stalls.

There was no response, but Roman paid no mind, his attention instead drawn to the open door in the back. Perhaps Jeremiah was finishing up some work outside. A couple of the horses were missing from their stalls. Jeremiah must still have them out in the corral.

With his eyes on the door, Roman rounded the corner past the last stall—and came to an abrupt halt. There was an obstacle in his path, something large and . . .

He squatted, holding up the lamp.

It was Jeremiah, sprawled out upon the straw and dirt.

Chapter Eighteen

CLARA AWOKE THE NEXT morning feeling just as irritated as she had been when she'd gone to sleep the night before. She understood Roman's reasoning—and a part of her truly appreciated his concern—but his rules were too much. As far as he was concerned, she might as well stay locked up here in the boardinghouse, where she'd be safe. But it felt like she'd been put in jail.

She flung off the bedcovers and began to dress. Roman couldn't understand that he'd be much better served if she was out, in town, talking and listening. Or even at the livery itself, speaking with customers. After all, the horse thieves were hardly going to attempt to conduct their crimes in broad daylight. And now that she'd seen, albeit from a distance, the two men who might very well be the ones behind the thefts, she might recognize them if they came into town.

Clara blinked at herself in the glass behind the washbasin before splashing water on her face. He hadn't said she couldn't leave the boardinghouse, only that he'd prefer if she left with company. That could certainly be accomplished. Abigail would be busy with her laundry, but Deirdre was often looking for ways to fill her time.

Clara forced herself not to race downstairs in her eagerness. She was determined to see what she could discover, and to prove to Roman that she was perfectly capable of taking care of herself. She found Deirdre eating breakfast with Abigail in the dining room. It didn't take much for Clara to convince Deirdre to accompany her, and so, after eating a slice of thick bread with honey, the two stepped out into town.

"Where shall we go first?" Deirdre asked.

"How about the mercantile?" Clara suggested. It was nearby, and besides, it would be nice to say hello to Caroline.

They arrived to find the little store nearly bursting at the seams. Mr. Drexel, Caroline's husband, helped people lined up at the counter in the rear of the store. Clara spotted Caroline assisting a well-dressed gentleman with a small selection of men's hats by the wall. When she finished, they rushed over to greet her.

"It's so good to see you both again," Caroline said with a friendly smile.

Clara warmed at her friend's welcome. It made Crest Stone feel more like home, having such good friends.

"I don't suppose you've heard anything of interest?" Clara asked.

"I haven't, but I did hear about what happened last night. I'm so sorry for Mr. Carlisle. I do hope the marshal can find out who's behind this."

"Last night?" Clara repeated. She looked to Deirdre, who appeared just as puzzled as Clara was.

"Yes . . ." Caroline trailed off, looking from Clara to Deirdre. "Oh my, you didn't know?"

Clara tensed. Something terrible had happened—to Roman—and here she was, prancing about town and knowing nothing about it.

"What didn't we know?" Deirdre asked.

Caroline glanced about them, and upon seeing no one nearby, continued. "Thomas made a delivery to Mr. Benton over at his shop, and Mr. Benton told him that the livery had been robbed again last night."

Clara's stomach dropped. "Was anyone hurt?"

"I don't know any more. I'm sorry, Clara. I shouldn't have said anything, but I thought you knew." Caroline's forehead crinkled in worry, and Clara reached out and laid a hand on her arm.

"It's quite all right. We'll go to the livery now. I'm glad you told me. If it happened late, there is no way I could have known." But even as she spoke the words, a sick feeling wound its way through her insides. She couldn't expect Roman to have paid her a visit first thing this morning, particularly when he had his hands full dealing with what had happened. But she should've *been* there, at the livery, right now. If she was to be his wife, she needed to be of help to him. He direly needed someone else at the livery, and he'd already told her how useful she'd been there. His fears for her working there during the day were completely unfounded. The thieves just proved again that they only came at night.

If she'd been there, she could be helping him, comforting him, right now instead of trying to collect wisps of gossip at the mercantile.

She turned and strode to the door, completely forgetting to bid Caroline goodbye. She vaguely heard Deirdre doing just that before catching up to her outside.

"I'm coming with you," Deirdre said, slipping an arm about Clara's.

Clara nodded. At least Roman couldn't complain that she'd walked about town alone, if she arrived with Deirdre in tow. Deirdre was somewhat shorter, and she had to step quickly to keep up, but Clara didn't slow.

She barely saw anyone as they walked, although her mind kept an eye out for a man in a red shirt and another all in brown. Not a soul matched those descriptions, but she wasn't surprised. They were likely on their way to wherever it was they would sell those horses, perhaps even to that man who'd cheated them out of a higher price.

Clara hoped he'd cheat them again. In fact, she hoped he robbed them blind. It was an un-Christian thought, but she didn't care. Not when Roman's business was on the line.

When they reached the livery, they had to step aside for a rather large man who was leaving. Clara recognized the banker, Mr. Gardiner. The man was not smiling—although she doubted he often was—but he seemed even more intimidating than usual as he left the stable. He didn't acknowledge them at all as he passed. If he'd just left without his horse, and his expression . . .

Clara closed her eyes quickly. Tartan. They must've gotten him. Her heart ached for the sweet horse with the white blaze who'd taken a liking to her. She squeezed her hands into fists and then let them go.

"Shall we go in?" Deirdre prompted.

Clara drew in a breath and slid through the open door, Deirdre following behind her. Inside, it took a second for her eyes to adjust. Even with the doors open, the stable was dim compared to the bright sunlight outside. When she could take in her surroundings, she saw Roman. He sat at the table, his head in his hands. Clara's anger at the thieves tempered into grief for the man she was to marry.

"I'll visit the horses," Deirdre whispered, gesturing toward the rear of the stable.

Clara nodded, and her friend quietly walked away.

"Roman?" she said quietly.

He looked up, letting his hands fall to the table. His eyes were dull, and his hair stood up at odd angles. Dark shadows ringed his eyes, and stubble dotted his chin. He looked as if he hadn't slept in days. "What are you doing here?" he asked, the life gone from his voice.

Clara stepped toward the desk, stopping beside it. "I came with a friend. I heard what happened."

He nodded, stretching a hand out along the desk and fidgeting with the edges of one of the ledgers.

"Tartan?" she asked.

"Along with another."

"I'm so sorry." Clara wanted to comfort him, to take him into her arms, to promise him the marshal would find out who'd done this and that they would pay dearly. She settled instead for resting a hand on top of his. He stopped fidgeting and looked at her hand for a second. Then, abruptly, he pulled it away and stood.

"They knocked Jeremiah out," he said, his back to her.

Clara put a hand over her mouth. "Is he all right?"

"He's fine," Roman said in a flat voice.

"How did they . . . Were you . . ." Clara wasn't certain how to ask how the men had gotten by Roman.

"I wasn't here." He turned back to face her, his face as dull as his words. "It happened before I returned last night."

"While you were walking me home," she said, the realization dawning that the men she'd seen had acted swiftly. Perhaps she hadn't fooled them after all.

"Or while I was speaking to the marshal at the hotel." Roman rubbed his face.

It was too much. The fact that those men had robbed him while he'd gone to the marshal about them was so terrible. It was the last thing he deserved, and Clara thought her heart might break in two. She rushed forward and threw her arms about him.

He stood still for a moment, as if he were frozen in place. And Clara froze too. The old fears tickled the edges of her mind. *He didn't want her. If she hadn't gone out and seen those men, he would've been here. She was driving him away the same way she drove Gideon away.*

Then, slowly, he lifted his arms and placed them around her, and Clara melted in relief. She would do anything for him, anything to keep this from happening again.

He held her close, his breath warm against her head. "I'm so sorry," he said.

"You have nothing to apologize for." She tilted her face up to see him.

He said nothing, but he held her gaze for a moment, just long enough for Clara to see the anguish there. Then, as if the scene had changed in a play and they were simply actors giving life to roles, he stiffened and stepped away.

"You need to go now," he said, not looking at her.

"Go?"

"Back to the Darbys'. Take your friend and stay there."

"But Roman, I'd rather stay with you. I can't help you if I'm not here. The thieves have proven they only come at night."

He looked at her then, his face cut like stone. "The only way you can help me is to stay at the boardinghouse. Out of the way."

Out of the way? Clara recoiled at his words.

"I wouldn't be in the way," she said, her voice smaller than she would have liked. "I can help with the customers while you and Mr. Wiley handle everything that's happened. You even said how useful I was here." *I could comfort you*, she thought.

"I was wrong. I don't have time for this nonsense. This is no place for you, Clara. I insist you return." He paced across the dirt and straw-covered floor and opened the front door. "Do you need me to escort you?"

"I do not," she said, as coolly as possible despite the emotions brewing inside of her. "However, Deirdre is in the back, and I must fetch her. We'll leave from there."

And with that, she turned so quickly her skirts flared out around her. She tromped past the empty stalls, hoping she kicked up enough dust to make Roman cough.

How dare he treat her like a child with no discernible use? How dare he speak to her in that manner! Clara pushed through the door in the rear of the stable and let it slam behind her.

"Whoa, Miss Brown. You'll scare the horses," Mr. Wiley said to her from beside the corral, where he stood with a smiling Deirdre.

"I apologize. Deirdre, we must leave now." Clara ground out the words, tears threatening to spill if she didn't keep herself together.

"Oh! All right." Deirdre's face was slightly flushed as she turned to Clara.

"Is everything well?" Mr. Wiley asked.

"Perfectly," Clara said, conjuring the words from some place inside that was still capable of normal conversation. "I'm sorry that you were hurt last night."

Mr. Wiley rubbed his head, his hat at his side. "Thank you, miss. It's nothing that won't heal."

"It was nice to meet you, Mr. Wiley," Deirdre said.

"Yes. Yes, it was good to meet you too, Miss Hannan." And to Clara's utter astonishment, Mr. Wiley's face went red as he returned his hat to his head.

They left from the corral, as the last thing Clara wanted to do was walk through the stable again.

"Mr. Wiley is awfully nice," Deirdre said as soon as they were past the livery.

Clara glanced at her friend. Deirdre was smiling at nothing, her blue eyes alight in the sun.

"He is," Clara replied. "I believe him to be a good man."

But despite her words, Deirdre must have heard something in her voice that belied her mood. "Did something happen between you and Mr. Carlisle?"

"He asked me to leave." That was all Clara could say, lest the tears that pricked at the backs of her eyes begin to fall.

"I'm certain he only wants you to remain safe," Deirdre said.

"Perhaps." Clara pondered Deirdre's words, but it certainly didn't feel that way. He'd simply asked her—no, *told* her—to leave. And that was before he'd said she was unhelpful and he wanted her out of the way.

What kind of wife could she be to him if he wouldn't let her stay nearby to help and provide comfort when he was in such distress? It was almost as if he didn't want a wife at all. Or he didn't want *her*.

Clara choked back a silent sob, determined not to worry Deirdre.

She had two choices: let the worry consume her whole, or prove to Roman how useful she could be. If he still didn't want her, well . . . she'd figure out what to do if that happened.

But right now, the sun was out, she had a good friend at her side, and Clara refused to let herself drown in fear. She'd make a good wife, and she'd ensure Roman knew it.

And she knew exactly how she would accomplish that—she would find those horse thieves.

Chapter Nineteen

IT WAS PAST NOON THE following day and the inaction was making Roman restless.

There wasn't much the marshal could do, not without some sort of lead. He'd been out to the creek, but there was no sign of the men Clara had seen. They were long gone, of course, with two stolen horses in tow. Wright said he'd alert the law in the mining encampment and in Cañon City, but Roman doubted that would do much.

He'd sold his last remaining rental horse, Georgia, yesterday, and then paid a visit to the banker. To Roman's surprise, the ornery man had not only said he'd continue to keep his carriage and second horse at the livery, but he also turned down Roman's offer of compensation for Tartan. And that was just as well, because the only way Roman could have paid for the second missing horse would be to sell his own mount, Thunder.

Then just that morning, two men had arrived early to retrieve their horses and stable them at the hotel livery instead.

Roman scowled as he passed the hotel on his way down to the creek. It wasn't the hotel's fault, not by any means. But he couldn't keep bleeding business away to them, not if he wanted to survive. He and Jeremiah could guard the livery from sunset to sunrise for the time being, but they couldn't do that forever. And it hadn't worked two nights ago.

He needed to find a way to stop these men.

He walked along the bank of the creek until he was in the general area where Clara had said she'd seen the men two days ago. There were remnants of a small fire and some horse manure, along with plenty of footprints. But that was all. Roman bit back a curse. What had he expected to find out here? The men's names and whereabouts written out?

He glared at the charred remains of the fire. So this was where they'd sat and plotted on how to steal his horses. Why him? Why hadn't they also targeted the hotel livery? It made no sense at all. If these were desperate men looking to sell stolen horses, why wouldn't they expand their reach? What was it about his stable that made it so easy to rob?

Perhaps he should pay another visit to the hotel livery and see what they had that he didn't. Was it extra men? Maybe they had several men out and armed at night. That would certainly be a deterrent. Or was it the location? He'd thought of that before. Being on the edge of town likely made him a target. The hotel livery was close enough to the hotel itself that perhaps its remote location atop the hill didn't matter. And yet, it sat much closer to this place by the creek than Roman's stable.

Roman sat on a large rock, staring out at the slow-moving water of Silver Creek. He needed more men, but had no way to pay them. As of right now, he couldn't even pay Jeremiah. It was up to him and Jeremiah, if his friend didn't up and find work elsewhere. And so far, they'd failed. How many more horses could he stand to lose before he no longer had a business?

He reached down to pitch a pebble into the water, his fingers closing around something metal instead. He lifted the item and brushed the mud from it.

It was a hair comb. A fancy one, with filigree and little shiny baubles like a woman concerned with her looks might wear.

And it looked oddly familiar.

Roman stood, staring at the thing in his hand. Clara had been nearby here, but he didn't think he'd seen her wear such a thing. She was far less given to ornate pieces such as this one.

He squinted at it as the metal caught the sunlight.

And then he remembered.

"Roman?"

He whirled about, half expecting to see his memory come to life behind him. But it was Clara.

Clara, who was down here, by herself, expressly defying what he'd told her to do to keep her safe. This headstrong woman was going to be the death of him.

You can't protect her, a voice whispered in his head. And as he glanced at the comb in his hand, he knew it was right. He couldn't protect her. He certainly couldn't provide for her, not with everything falling apart as he looked on. He was utterly helpless.

Why he'd ever thought he could be anything like his brothers, he didn't know. He never would be, that much he was sure of at this point.

It was time he faced that fact. And moved on.

Chapter Twenty

TIME SLOWED AS ROMAN stared at whatever it was that he held in his hand. Clara dug her fingers into her palms, waiting for him to acknowledge her. He'd be mad, of that much she was certain. But she wasn't entirely alone. Deirdre had come with her, but had turned her ankle just beyond the trees. Clara had reassured her she would be fine, and Deirdre waited for her while she rested her ankle.

Although she supposed that meant she *was* alone. And not only was she alone, she was far from the boardinghouse. And in a place he'd specifically told her not to go.

She ought to have turned and snuck away, but she couldn't simply leave him here, looking so bereft. She'd explain to him what she was doing, and maybe—hopefully—he would understand. He couldn't fault her for wanting to help him in any way she could.

Could he?

Clara prayed harder than she ever had before. "Roman," she said again.

He finally looked up at her, but although he saw her, his eyes seemed to be seeing something else entirely. As if he were somewhere far away.

Clara gathered her courage. "I know you told me to stay at the boardinghouse, but I thought that maybe if I came here, I might be able to find something . . . I—I'm not alone. Deirdre is just beyond the trees."

He closed his eyes, not responding, his hand clenched around the item he held.

"I wanted to help," she continued. "A wife is supposed to be a help to her husband."

He flinched as if she'd struck him. Clara bit her lip, wishing he'd say something.

After a moment stretched between them, one in which Clara thought the birdsong in the trees overhead would drive her mad, he finally spoke.

"This is a hair comb," he said, opening his hand to show Clara a muddy thing that was once a very beautiful—and expensive—piece of jewelry for the hair. It was far nicer than anything Clara had ever owned. She couldn't imagine wearing such a thing.

She wasn't certain what she was supposed to say, and so she nodded.

He looked at it as he spoke. "I've seen this very comb before, almost two years ago. A man I worked with, a friend at that time, purchased it for a woman he was courting. A Miss Ethel Porter.

"I can't forget it, because I'd wondered how Hoskins had come into the money for it. This little thing cost far more than we made running cattle, and he'd bought a pair of them. I asked him how he'd paid for it, and he gave me this . . . look. And that's when I knew. Or at least, I suspected."

He looked up at Clara finally, his eyes seemingly seeing her for the first time since she'd stumbled upon him. She caught her breath, waiting for the rest of the story.

"And then I found out for certain. He and another fellow, Thaddeus Jones, had been siphoning off the herd we were being paid to round up and take to Denver. They were selling the cattle—I don't know to whom—but making a pretty penny doing it."

"What happened?" Clara asked quietly when he paused.

His face darkened. "I can't abide dishonesty. Particularly when it puts the livelihood of so many men at risk. I gave them the opportunity to leave, but they refused."

"You turned them in," Clara said.

He nodded, glancing at the comb again. "They were none too happy, as you can imagine. The sheriff kept them in the local jail for a while, but they couldn't ever bring enough evidence against them to do anything about it. Of course, that rancher made sure word got around. I doubt they've been able to work since then."

Clara drew in a deep breath. "But they're here."

"So it appears." He clenched the comb in his fist and dropped it to his side. "And it all makes sense now, what's happening."

"If you know who they are, you can tell Marshal Wright. At least now he'll know who to search for." A spark of hope lit inside of Clara. They had names! It was so much more than they'd had before.

"It won't matter. They're long gone by now. And when they return, they'll be smart about it." Roman's face darkened.

"We'll tell the town. Everyone likes you. Surely they'll agree to help keep watch for them."

"No one is going to sit up, night after night, unless I pay them." He ran a hand over his face. "I'm done for, Clara, don't you understand? It's over."

She stepped forward and grabbed hold of his hand, desperate for him to believe there was still hope. "It isn't. This is what you've wanted, and I *know* you, Roman. You're strong enough to make it through this."

He laughed, but the sound was empty. "I'm not. Not without money. Not without the promise this won't happen again." He let go of her hand and stepped away. "The sale of the wagon and a couple of the saddles ought to pay for your fare home."

"My fare . . ." His words rang in her ears. "No, I don't understand."

"I can't marry you." He wouldn't look at her.

Clara stepped around him, trying to catch his eye. Finally, he looked at her, but all she saw was the hollowed-out version of Roman. "Money doesn't matter to me."

"It should. You're a fool if you believe otherwise." His words were cold, and Clara bristled.

"You don't believe that."

Roman turned empty eyes toward her. "I do. Go back to the boardinghouse, Miss Brown. I'll get the money tomorrow and you can be on your way."

Clara pinched her lips together to keep them from trembling. He didn't want her help. He didn't even want her nearby. And now he was sending her away so he could . . . what?

She couldn't stand there any longer with him looking at her in that way. Clara gathered her skirts and lifted her chin, willing herself not to shed a tear in his presence. But just before she turned, his stiff veneer cracked, and she saw, just for a millisecond, a sadness that sat behind it. But when she looked again, it was gone.

Had she imagined it? She didn't know, but she certainly couldn't stand here and let him push her away any longer. He'd decided he didn't want her, and she needed to take that to heart and leave now.

Before he could hurt her more than he already had.

She'd return home and nurse her heartbreak there. At least she'd still have her dignity intact.

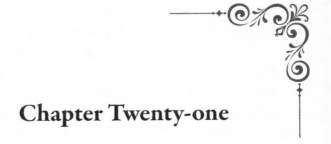

Chapter Twenty-one

IT WAS TWO DAYS BEFORE Roman could sell enough to pay for a one-way fare home for Clara, and then it was only enough for a partial journey by train. She'd have to take a stage for part of the way. The money in his hand felt like utter failure. He didn't know what he'd write to his parents, and right then, he didn't much care. All he could picture was living every day like this one—without Clara.

But he didn't deserve her. Not if he couldn't afford to finish building the roof to put over her head, and certainly not if he couldn't keep the livery in business. He wasn't capable of living a settled life—that's what he should have known all along, and it was clear to him now. At least he could afford to send her home, back to the life she once had. Surely there was a man in Virginia who could marry and provide for her.

Roman crumpled the bills in his hand. It was for the best, despite the jealousy that arose when he thought of this unnamed, unknown man. He was doing what was right for Clara, whether she believed it to be or not.

She was angry with him, so much so she hadn't bothered to seek him out since he'd sent her back to the boardinghouse that afternoon by the creek. Sweet Clara, with her optimism overflowing so much that she generally ignored whatever rule he'd set down in place of believing the best. Except this time. She hadn't been by the livery at all, never mind about town. Had he squashed that confidence from her for good?

He hoped not. But perhaps he'd at least displaced any notion she'd had that he was the man for her. He'd rather send her home angry and disappointed than see her shivering and hungry a year from now because he was incapable of doing anything other than running cattle.

It was better this way.

And at some point his heart would begin to believe that too.

"Mr. Carlisle?" Young Christopher Rennet stood over him, clutching an envelope in his hand.

Roman blinked at the boy. He'd been out here for so long the sun had sunk in the sky and the evening chill had set in. Another sleepless night of sitting awake and waiting for men from his past, rifle in his lap, yawned ahead. "Yes?" he finally said to Christopher.

"A letter for you." The kid held out the wrinkled envelope.

Roman stared at it a moment before taking it. Mr. Thomason wasn't in the habit of delivering mail, instead keeping it at the depot post office until one stopped by to collect it. The envelope itself was blank, without even a name. "Did Thomason send you with this?"

"No, sir. I was on my way to get some supper when a fellow asked me to deliver this to you. He paid me." The kid held up a coin with a grin.

Roman tore the letter open, praying with all his might it wasn't yet another customer notifying him that he'd be taking his horse up to the hotel livery. He unfolded the paper inside to find feminine penmanship—one that he'd seen lately in his ledger books.

My Dear Mr. Carlisle,

Please meet me by the creek as soon as possible. You will know where. I have something important to show you.

Yours,

Miss Brown

"What did the man look like?" Roman asked, jerking his head up to find that Christopher had already left. He stood, his gaze returning to the words in his hand. It was her writing, of that much he was certain. But why would she write to him instead of simply coming by the livery, particularly if she were already brushing aside his insistence—again—that she remain at the boardinghouse? It made no sense. And then—

"Roman?" Jeremiah stood in the doorway, his hat pushed back to reveal a mess of hair and a face that looked as if it needed a month's worth of sleep. "You eat yet?"

Roman shook his head slowly, glancing down at the letter before handing it to Jeremiah. "What do you make of that?"

Jeremiah read it out loud, slowly, then looked up at Roman. "Sounds as if the lady wishes you to meet her by the creek." He waggled his eyebrows and grinned.

Roman frowned. "I'm sending her home."

"Now why would you go and do a thing like that?" Jeremiah's usually cheerful countenance fell.

"I can't marry her, Jeremiah." Roman read the letter again, trying to discern what felt off about it, besides its very presence.

"Why not? She's a good girl, friendly and kind. And she likes horses," Jeremiah replied, as if that was all that mattered. "And strangely enough, she likes you too."

"Our business is falling apart, if you haven't noticed," Roman said shortly. "I can't take on the responsibility of a wife if I can't ensure she's provided for."

"It ain't falling apart."

Roman looked up from the letter to find Jeremiah staring him down. He threw out his hand, the letter bending in the breeze. "What do you call it then? We've lost how many horses? Whether to thieves or the fear of theft, it doesn't matter. I can't afford to keep running the place if we have no customers."

Jeremiah crossed his arms and regarded Roman for a moment. "I suppose you're right. But I choose to look at it as a momentary setback. Those fellas will get themselves caught and strung up soon enough. We'll persevere. So long as you don't give up, anyhow. And I think you're a fool to let that woman go because you're afraid."

A fool. That was precisely what he'd told Clara she'd been. He winced at the memory. He'd said that to push her away, but perhaps he hadn't needed to be so cruel.

"I'm not afraid," Roman growled.

Jeremiah held his gaze. "The letter," he finally said. "It's odd she called you Mr. Carlisle, considering I've heard her call you by your Christian name on more than one occasion."

Roman looked at the paper again. Jeremiah was right. She'd addressed and signed her letter formally, as if they barely knew each other. Then again, he *had* called her Miss Brown the other evening, hoping to indicate to her that whatever was between them was over. Perhaps she was only doing the same.

He didn't know what to make of it.

"Is it real?" Jeremiah finally asked. When Roman gave him a questioning look, he added, "The letter."

"I don't know. It's her handwriting, so I imagine it is."

"Why wouldn't she simply come here?" Jeremiah's question—the same as Roman's—lingered in the cool air. The setting sun cast the corral beside them in warm hues of pink and gold as something cold and terrifying settled in Roman's bones.

"You don't suppose . . ." he began. Had someone forced her to write this letter to lure him to the creek? Or was he reading too much into it?

Jeremiah appeared to be just as confused as Roman. "I don't know, but you should go. Just be smart about it."

Roman nodded. Jeremiah was right. Hoskins and Jones were men bent on revenge. He couldn't imagine they'd want to harm Clara, but he also never imagined they'd track him down and destroy his livelihood. If they had her, it was him they really wanted. He'd arrive prepared.

"Get Benton to watch the place with you while I'm gone," Roman said, the letter crumpling in his hand.

"You going to stop for the marshal on the way?" Jeremiah asked as Roman made his way to the door.

"No time." If Hoskins and Jones really had Clara, Roman wasn't about to detour up the hill to the hotel when he could be handling the situation. And if they didn't, and Clara was alone by the creek waiting for him in defiance of everything he'd told her to do . . .

He'd never hoped so much for a defiant woman.

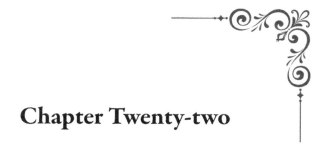

Chapter Twenty-two

THE MAN—JONES, THE other one had called him—smelled of stale whiskey and sweat. Clara sat as straight as she could on the horse to keep from touching him as they waited a distance away from the livery.

The sun had dipped below the horizon, hidden by the mountains, when they saw Roman leave.

"Suppose we didn't need to bring her after all," Jones said, his breath much too close to the back of her neck.

"She could still be useful for persuading the other fellow," the bigger man on the other horse said. Red was what the woman back at their camp had called him. She was on mighty friendly terms with Red. Clara supposed she was the one the comb belonged to—Miss Porter—and that Red was the same person that Roman had referred to as Hoskins.

Clara clenched her fingers to keep from trembling at Hoskins's words. She didn't know exactly what they meant, and if she thought about it, it would only serve to distract her from what she needed to do. So instead, she watched Roman.

He rode, rather than walked, and took off quickly toward the south. That letter the thieves made her write had worked, despite her hope that it wouldn't. Perhaps she should have left more obvious clues in the letter, but it was too late now.

Instead, she found herself waiting on a horse some ways away from the livery with two thieves. They'd found her behind the boardinghouse a few hours ago, when she'd gone outside to hang clothing she'd helped Abigail wash. She'd been hidden behind some of the bed linens Abigail had hung earlier when they approached. They hadn't wasted a lick of time with trying to lure her away. Instead, Hoskins had simply pulled a pistol and told her to come with them.

Clara had plenty of time since to wonder what else she could have done in that moment—screamed, ran, pretended to faint dead away. Instead, her heart in her throat, she'd let the tall, leaner Jones grab hold of her arm and lead her away.

She'd make up for her mistake somehow, she decided as they'd taken her with them to a little camp at the base of a hill just east of town. She wouldn't let these men destroy the little Roman had left. The letter had been a failure, as had her attempt to escape while they'd spoken to Miss Porter. They'd caught her with embarrassing ease, and since then, she'd thought of nothing other than how else she could stop their plans.

Because despite the fact that Roman insisted on sending her back East, she couldn't let him give up entirely. He might not want her, but he deserved something good in his life. She owed him that much for the adventure he'd given her here—and for the way he'd made her feel, for at least a short time. She could live the rest of her life a spinster, if she knew he had his horses and his livery. At least then she could rely on her memories—and the knowledge that he was still here in Crest Stone, living the life he'd worked so hard for—to keep her going.

And perhaps he'd tell her *why* before she left. If she knew what defect existed in her character, she could make peace with it. He owed her at least that much, to tell her what it was.

But first, she would save his business.

"Ready?" the foul-smelling fellow behind her asked his partner.

"Let's move," Hoskins replied. He was the leader, she'd figured that much out in the few hours she'd been with them. She wished she could have discovered how they'd found Roman, two years after everything had happened at that ranch.

With a kick to the horse, they were moving toward the livery. A million different scenarios played through Clara's mind. She could fall off the horse. She could somehow alert Jeremiah, who she imagined was still inside the stable. Or if she aimed just right, she could elbow Jones hard in the stomach.

Indecision raged through her as they grew closer. With Roman gone, only Mr. Wiley remained to defend the livery. These men hadn't hesitated to knock him out the last time they'd come. Clara prayed they wouldn't do worse this time.

As they rode up to the corral, Clara was relieved to see it was empty. Although that also meant they would need to force their way into the stable if they went through with their plans.

"Hold it right there." Mr. Wiley's voice boomed from somewhere nearby. In the darkness, Clara couldn't see exactly where he was, but she'd certainly never heard the affable Mr. Wiley sound so threatening.

The men drew up their horses, much to Clara's relief. If it was too dark for Clara to see Mr. Wiley, chances were that he couldn't make out exactly who was on the horses in front of him.

"It would be in the best interest of this young lady if you put down your gun and let us take what we came here for," Hoskins said from the horse next to Clara and Jones.

As if on cue, Jones slid a pistol from his holster and held it against Clara's side. She gasped, and he clamped a hand around her arm.

"Relax," Jones whispered. "I ain't going to shoot you. So long as this fellow does as Red says, anyhow." He chuckled, low and quiet, and Clara tried unsuccessfully to wrench her arm out of his grip.

"What young lady?" Mr. Wiley asked, and Clara knew for certain he couldn't see who was on the horses.

Before Hoskins could answer, the smaller door to the stable opened, and a lantern inside illuminated Mr. Benton, the blacksmith, holding a shotgun. The light spilled out, showing Mr. Wiley just by the door, pointing a rifle at them.

If Mr. Benton's presence alarmed the thieves at all, they didn't show it. Jones still held fast to Clara, the muzzle of his pistol in her side. And Hoskins sat back on his horse, seemingly unconcerned.

"Miss Brown?" Mr. Wiley said as the door shut behind Mr. Benton, sending them back into darkness.

"We collected Miss Brown outside her boardinghouse earlier today," Hoskins said, his voice light as if he were telling a story. "Say something, Miss Brown, so these good men will know you're all right."

Clara clamped her lips shut. The last thing she wanted was to help these men with their plans.

"Say something," Jones growled in her ear, his fingers digging into her arm.

"Mr. Wiley," she squeaked. "I'm here." She hated herself for giving in to what these men wanted. She was supposed to be figuring out a way to stop them, not helping them along.

Hoskins leaned forward on his horse, and Clara could almost see him smiling. "If you'd like Miss Brown to survive this encounter, then I suggest you set down your weapons and open up that big door."

A moment passed, one in which Clara didn't dare take a breath. She was more aware than ever before of the presence of the pistol against her side, and yet despite that, she could hardly stand to see Mr. Wiley and Mr. Benton comply with these horrible men's demands.

And yet they did. As the larger door—the one used for the horses and the wagon—opened, the lantern light from inside illuminated Mr. Wiley and Mr. Benton, scowling and standing with their guns on the ground.

Without a word, both thieves dismounted. Jones held out a hand to Clara. She glared at him before taking it. She didn't have much of a choice, given that he was still holding that pistol.

Hoskins collected the discarded weapons before ushering Mr. Wiley and Mr. Benton inside the stable. Jones pressed Clara along, grabbing hold of her arm again as he led the horses in behind him.

Inside the stable, Hoskins had taken the lamp and was already moving along the row of stalls, examining each horse. At the end of the row, he turned back to them. "We're taking them all," he announced.

Clara's heart fell.

"But how—" Jones began.

"Tie them together. Let's get this done with," Hoskins replied.

"You can't do that," Clara said, her voice rising with emotion. "You'll put Roman and Mr. Wiley out of business."

The grin on Hoskins's face made Clara shiver. "That's why we're here, little lady. We owe Carlisle a little taste of what he gave us. Thaddeus and I ain't had legitimate work since he smeared our names from here to Denver."

Roman had been right—it *was* personal.

"Lock them up, but keep her out here. We may need her if Carlisle returns," Hoskins said, his attention already turned back to the horses. "These ones should fetch a good amount."

Jones waved his pistol at Mr. Benton and Mr. Wiley. They both stood rooted to the floor, Mr. Benton looking mean enough to spit and Mr. Wiley angrier than Clara ever thought possible. When they didn't move, Jones shoved Clara in front of him, almost like a threat.

They slowly made their way to the room where the saddles and rope and other equipment was kept. Normally Clara loved that room, with its heady scent and shining leather, but all she felt right now was guilt as Jones ordered the men to toss out halters and lead ropes for the horses. If she hadn't let the thieves grab hold of her at the boardinghouse, Mr. Wiley and Mr. Benton would've had a fighting chance. They'd given up to keep her safe.

They were giving up *everything* for her.

Clara bit down hard on her lip. Going to pieces was the easy choice. But it wouldn't help anything. As Jones locked the men into the room, she knew she was the only one left who could save the livery.

Roman might not want her, but she'd prove to him exactly what he'd miss by sending her away.

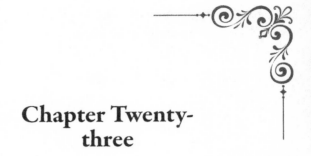

Chapter Twenty-three

THERE WASN'T A SOUL near Silver Creek.

Roman had stood there on the bank, breathing hard after that ride, as it all began to make sense. They weren't luring him here to kill him. They were getting him out of the way.

And Clara was likely with them.

He ran back toward where he'd left Thunder tied to a tree. They would use Clara to gain access to the livery. It wouldn't have mattered how many men Jeremiah had gotten to help guard the place. If Red Hoskins and Thaddeus Jones rode up with Clara in tow, threatening her life, they'd step aside.

Branches smacked his arms and face as he strode through the trees, but Roman hardly noticed. All he could see in his head was a frightened Clara, a victorious sneer on Hoskins's face, and Jeremiah and Benton, helpless to do anything to protect Clara or the horses. Why had he fallen for it? He'd seen the most obvious option—the one they'd wanted him to see—and left Clara vulnerable.

As he emerged from the trees, he knew one thing for certain: he'd give up every horse and every penny he had to see Clara protected. Hoskins and Jones hadn't been given to violence until Roman had confronted them about their cattle rustling operation. He involuntarily ran a finger over the scar above his lip, and the memories resurfaced as if they'd happened yesterday. He'd told them he knew what they were doing and offered to let them leave. If they went, he'd keep their misdeeds to himself. They'd been his friends, or so he'd thought, and the idea of going to the sheriff, or to the owners of the ranches from which they'd stolen, left a bad taste in his mouth. He'd thought for certain they'd be thankful, and that they'd be gone by morning.

But instead, Hoskins had drawn a knife and lunged at him. Roman had fought him off, but not before the man had sliced his face. They didn't leave. Not that night or the next day.

And so Roman had gone to the sheriff.

They were promptly arrested, and although they'd never stood trial, their names were as good as mud when it came to any rancher in this part of Colorado. He hadn't seen them in almost two years. He had no idea what they were capable of now.

And they had Clara.

Roman eased the horse forward, and as he did, it was as if cobwebs had been swept from his mind.

He loved her.

The realization was so obvious he didn't know how he hadn't seen it before. But he'd done the right thing, hadn't he? Even if he did love her, even if she meant everything to him, it would be wrong to trap her here with him when he couldn't give her anything approaching a comfortable life.

Except she hadn't agreed with that at all. Had she been right? Or was she simply blind to the facts?

Roman didn't know, but he pressed Thunder on, back into town, past the Darbys' boardinghouse, past the saloon, past the hotel up on the hill. If he had more time, he'd get Marshal Wright. But time was the one thing he didn't have right now.

He pulled up by the smithy's and tied the horse there. His heart hammering, he reached for the revolver he'd brought with him. With it firmly in hand, he crept around the rear of the blacksmith's toward the stable.

From the outside, all appeared to be quiet. Not a sound came from inside as Roman silently stepped along the wall. The smaller door was closed, but one of the larger doors was wide open. Roman raised the revolver as he approached.

He paused just beside the door. Hooves shuffled against the straw-covered floor inside. And then a man's voice—Red Hoskins, he was certain—shouted to hold a horse steady.

Roman drew in a deep breath, redoubled his grip on the revolver, and peered around the edge of the doorway. A single lamp illuminated the scene before him. Horses—nearly half of those currently stabled at the livery—stood nearby, all tethered together. He could see neither Hoskins nor Jones, but there—he squinted into the shadows—there was Clara. She stood awkwardly in front of one of the first stalls, and appeared to be working frantically at something that held her wrist to the stall door.

Jeremiah and Benton were nowhere in sight, and Roman took that as a good sign. If Hoskins and Jones had shot them, surely it would have happened here, near the entrance to the stable. Not to mention that half the town would have heard the gunshots.

He pulled back around the corner, deciding on a plan of action. He was one man against two—he had to assume so, anyhow. He was armed, but so were they. All he had on his side was the element of surprise. If he could enter by the front, silently, he could sneak up on them.

It was his only option.

Mind made up, he slid sideways. He'd taken exactly one step when a shout sounded from inside. A split second later, hooves pounded against the floor of the stable, and no less than ten horses ran from the door out into the night.

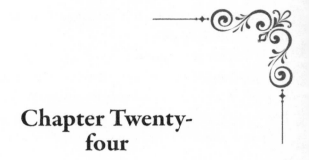

Chapter Twenty-four

"GRAB HER!" HOSKINS shouted as he snagged one of the horses that hadn't yet been tied to the others.

Clara didn't wait. She ran for the door behind the horses she'd scared off, the rope dangling from her wrist. Just as she reached the door, a hand grabbed hold of her and pulled her through.

"Roman!" she gasped as he moved her behind him. He didn't have a chance to speak a word, because just at that moment, Jones burst through the door.

Roman barreled into him, knocking the man to the ground and the guns from both their hands. Clara took a step backward as Roman landed a fist against Jones's face. Hoskins would still be inside, trying to gather and calm the remaining loose horses, but it wouldn't be long before he'd emerge in search of Jones—or see what was happening right outside the door.

Roman needed help—now.

She darted past the men as Roman shouted her name. She ignored him, racing into the stable. She glanced toward the stalls. Hoskins had hold of a stallion, who appeared none too happy to have a halter on after the other horses had gone running from the stable. He didn't see her as she ran to the room with Mr. Wiley and Mr. Benton. She yanked on the doorknob, remembering almost immediately that it was locked.

The key. Where had Jones put the key? Clara leaned her head against the door, unable to remember.

"Mr. Wiley!" she said as loudly as she dared. "Is there another key?"

"Roman has the other," came the reply.

Clara sagged against the door. She could hardly ask him to toss her a key right now. Unless she could help him subdue Jones. But how could she do that? It was too dark outside to see where their pistols had fallen. If there were a shovel or some other tool, perhaps she could strike him. She looked frantically about the stable.

Something metal glinted in the lamplight, beyond where Hoskins struggled with the horse. Clara blinked at it, hardly believing they were there. She'd been so preoccupied with freeing her wrist from the door earlier, she hadn't even noticed them. Glancing at Hoskins, she flew across to the last stall in the row on the wall. She picked up Mr. Benton's shotgun. She hadn't the slightest idea how to use it, but Jones didn't know that.

"Hey!" Hoskins shouted from a few yards away.

Clara jerked around, the shotgun heavy in her hands. Just as Hoskins started to take a step forward, the stallion reared up on its hind legs, knocking him to the ground.

Clara didn't wait to see if he stirred. She made for the door, emerging into the night where she found the two men standing and Roman clutching the side of his face. She couldn't see the state of them in the darkness, but Jones stumbled backward, unsteady. He righted himself and started toward Roman again.

"Stop right there!" Clara yelled. Her heart pounded in her ears as she raised the shotgun and aimed it at Jones.

It took him by surprise—and Roman too. Roman stared at her for a second, before taking advantage of Jones's stunned state and slamming a fist into the man's stomach.

Jones crumpled to the ground as Roman moved quickly and scooped up both his revolver and Jones's. He held one aloft, pointed at Jones, who didn't move.

"I didn't know you could shoot," he said, his breath coming fast, as he moved back to stand near Clara.

"I can't," she said, letting the shotgun drop. Now that Roman was safe from Jones, the thing felt as heavy as a horse in her hands.

Roman stared at her a moment, a grin slowly moving the corners of his lips upward before he grimaced in pain.

"Are you hurt?" Clara asked, straining to see the finer details of his face in the darkness.

"Nothing that won't heal."

"The other man is still inside. I don't know if he's conscious," she said.

Roman's eyes widened. "What did you do to him?"

"It wasn't me. It was that stallion."

"Granger's? I knew I liked that beast."

As if he'd heard himself mentioned, the stallion appeared in the doorway, seemingly calm now that he'd gotten Hoskins out of the way.

"Good boy," Roman said, stroking the horse on the nose as he kept the pistol trained on Jones. He peered into the stable. "He's still down."

Clara let out a deep breath. "They locked Mr. Wiley and Mr. Benton in that room." She pointed inside the stable.

Roman placed Jones's pistol in the holster he wore and pulled a key from his pocket. "Why don't you let them out, and then we can take these two up to the marshal."

Clara took the key from him. "There's a woman at their camp."

"Miss Porter," Roman said. "I can't believe she stood by Hoskins."

"I think she was helping. Perhaps they're in love," Clara said. Her words sat between them, heavy, and she almost wished she could take them back. But Roman didn't look away. Not entirely sure what to think of that, Clara made her way inside the livery and let the other men out of the locked room. She happily handed Mr. Benton back his shotgun when he emerged. She'd be grateful to never need to handle one again, although, she decided, it might not be such a bad idea to learn how to actually use it. Perhaps it was something Roman could teach her.

She squeezed her eyes closed as the men managed to awaken Hoskins after tying his hands. Here she was, assuming Roman had seen how helpful she could be and had changed his mind about her.

And assuming her heart could trust him again after he'd summarily decided to send her away.

She stood quietly aside as they rounded up the escaped horses, none of which had gone very far, and then helped return each horse to its stall. She was rubbing the nose of one particularly pretty white horse when Mr. Wiley and Mr. Benton offered to take the thieves to the marshal.

"It's best if I talk to Wright, since I know these two," Roman said. "Besides, I need to let him know they've got Miss Porter as an accomplice back at their camp."

"Mrs. Hoskins," Hoskins, who was apparently her husband, spat at Roman. "We're married."

"Congratulations," Roman said, his voice flat. "I doubt you'll spend much time together in prison."

Hoskins looked as if he was ready to say more, but Mr. Wiley cut him off.

"You can talk to Wright later. We'll let him know about the woman. Besides," Mr. Wiley said with a glance at Clara. "I think you're needed here."

Roman frowned and Clara looked away, her heart sinking. She'd proven nothing at all.

He still wanted nothing to do with her.

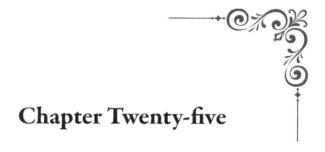

Chapter Twenty-five

ROMAN WATCHED BENTON and Jeremiah leave with Hoskins and Jones in tow. He had a million things to say to the men who'd stolen his horses, but none were more important than what he needed to tell Clara.

When he could finally see them no longer, he shut the door at the front of the stable and turned.

Clara had gone one by one down the stalls, soothing the horses by talking gently to each one and petting them on the neck and the nose. She stood in front of Granger's stallion now, saying something in her sweet voice that Roman couldn't hear.

He hadn't had much time to think on what he'd figured out down by the creek earlier, but now it all came rushing back to him.

He loved her.

The thought of losing her, of sending her home, left a hole inside that he could never fill. But his future was uncertain. It would be selfish of him to hold her here—to marry her—when he didn't know what kind of life he could give her. The thieves had been caught, but whether or not his business was still viable, he didn't know.

And if it was, was he capable of running it?

The only thing he knew for certain was that he had to speak with her. He'd lay out the facts, and perhaps she'd see reason—even if it killed him in the process.

"I believe if he's treated kindly, he'll be a gentle sort of horse," Clara said, her voice like honey, low and sweet, as she ran a hand down the stallion's nose.

Roman swallowed and looked at the horse. "Perhaps." Why did she have to be so good with the horses? It made all of this so much harder.

"Clara," he finally said.

She glanced at him, her eyes skeptical. Had he done that? She'd arrived here so full of hope and joy, and all he'd done was promise her marriage—and then push her away.

No wonder she didn't trust him.

"Clara," he said again, trying to summon the courage to be honest with her.

She clasped her hands together and looked at the ground. "I know you don't want me. I won't try to persuade you to change your mind. I can leave tomorrow, if that's feasible."

"No," he said, more forcefully than he'd intended.

She jerked her head up, her forehead wrinkled in confusion.

He closed his eyes briefly. "You should go. But it isn't because I don't want you. God help me, I want you too much." His voice caught in his throat, emotions threatening to spill over. It took every ounce of energy he had not to reach for her and crush her into his arms. "And that's why I want you to leave."

"I . . . I don't understand."

"I don't know what's going to happen here. This entire business could be over with tomorrow or next week. Or it might not. But even if folks continue to board their horses here, I don't know . . . I don't know if I can do this." It hurt to put words to the doubts that had sat deeply inside him for so long. The same doubts that had prevented him from doing anything worthwhile for years. The ones that had him convinced he'd never be anything more than a drifter, doomed to fail at everything he attempted.

"Of course you can run the livery," Clara said. She straightened, her face more determined than Roman had ever seen. "You have a talent with horses, and you get along well with people. In the short time I've been here, I haven't met a person who didn't have good things to say about you."

Roman didn't know what to say to that. Sure, he got along with folks, but he didn't think anyone really held him in much high esteem. He was, after all, just a cowboy trying to create a legitimate business.

"I don't know what your parents or your brothers might have said to you to make you think you can't make something wonderful out of your life, but they're wrong. You can, Roman. I know you can." She held his gaze, wisps of her bright hair framing her beautiful face.

Her words reached his ears and settled inside, melting away the obstacles that had stood in his path. He was ambitious enough to build this place and ask folks to stable their horses here. There was nothing at all to keep him from coming back after Hoskins and Jones's attempt to sabotage it all. Nothing at all, except his own doubts.

Roman swallowed. She was right.

He drew his hands together behind him. "You have my word that I'll do everything in my power to make this place succeed. But Clara . . ." His eyes searched hers. He didn't know what he was looking for, but something about the way she looked at him gave him courage. "I can't keep you here. I can't force you into something that might not succeed."

She gave him a sad smile. "You wouldn't be forcing me into anything."

"What do you mean?"

Clara took a step toward him, so close he could feel the warmth of her presence. Roman clenched his hands together. She turned her sweet face up to him, and he thought he'd never seen anything so completely pure and honest in his life.

"I love you, Roman Carlisle. I want to stay here. Not because I believe you'll be a wildly successful livery man—although I do believe that to be true. But because I want to be with you. I don't care if it's hard, or if you own a livery or nothing at all. I want to be with *you*." Her eyes darted down quickly. "If that's what you want."

He stared at her a moment. She loved him. Those simple words repeated themselves in his head, over and over, until he started to believe they were true.

And then he could stand it no longer, having her this close to him and not touching her. He drew a hand to her chin, lifting it so he could see her face.

"I love you, Clara." He drew in a deep breath, relishing the feel of her skin beneath his hand. "I don't deserve anyone as perfect as you. Someone who believes in me so wholeheartedly."

She gazed at him with eyes gray in the dim light of the stable. He moved his hand to her cheek, and she pressed into his touch, closing her eyes briefly.

"I want to marry you so badly, but I . . ." Doubt reared its ugly head again, taking the words from him.

"Roman." Clara pressed her hand over his. "Please, just ask me. Again."

He ran his thumb over her cheekbone. "Are you sure?"

"Roman." She looked at him now with undisguised impatience.

A laugh threatened deep inside him. Roman shook his head, trying not to grin in such a serious moment. "Clara, would you marry me?"

"Of course. After all, didn't I agree already down by the creek some time ago?"

Her wide eyes and mischievous smile made him laugh, out loud this time. "You enjoyed that, didn't you?" He lifted his free hand to cradle her other cheek, and then dipped his head to kiss the grin from her face.

A soft sigh escaped her lips as he met them with his. If this incredible, brave, beautiful woman believed in him, then nothing so small as men seeking revenge could stop him from building the life he wanted.

Roman moved a hand to press Clara closer to him. She responded by wrapping her arms around him, her small hands pressing into his back. She was as sweet as a summer breeze and completely perfect. And she was his.

They could do anything, together.

Epilogue

SEPTEMBER 1876

Slices of ham sizzled in the pan on the stove. That, along with the potatoes keeping warm next to them and the leftover slices of last night's apple pie, would make a good, hearty noon meal for Roman, Jeremiah, and the young man they'd recently hired to help out at the livery. While the ham cooked, Clara glanced about the kitchen and smiled. It was perfect.

In fact, everything about her little home with Roman was perfect. There were still a few pieces of furniture she wished to add—a couple more chairs for the kitchen table, a small table for the parlor, and a wardrobe for their clothing—but they had everything they needed. Somehow, after the thieves—and Mrs. Hoskins, who the marshal had found at the camp east of town where the men had kept Clara—were caught and sent up to Cañon City, word had gotten around town that Roman and Clara were waiting to marry until he had time to finish their house. Over the next few days, men of all sorts had shown up at the livery, tools in hand and ready to help. The house was completed within the week, and they had the furniture they needed a week after that. Even better, the men in town had trusted Roman again with their horses, and his business was doing better than it ever had before.

Clara added ham and potatoes to three plates, along with a slice of pie. She'd just finished covering the last plate with a napkin when the kitchen door opened and Roman appeared.

"Something smells good," he said. He crossed the room and lifted the napkin from one of the plates, then gave her a serious look. "I don't believe Jeremiah or Fred care much for pie."

Clara smiled and swatted him with the apron she'd just untied. "You only say that because you want to eat it all yourself."

"Can you blame me?" He took the apron from her and tossed it onto a chair, before wrapping his arms about her waist.

She gave him an appraising look. "Hmm . . ."

He broke into a grin, making the scar over his lip disappear, and Clara thought—not for the first time—that she'd be content simply to make him smile for the rest of her life.

"I wrote to my parents," he said. "Just this morning."

"Oh?"

"I sent them the photograph we had taken and invited them to pay us a visit. I doubt they'll come, but do you know what I realized when I posted the letter?" He paused, his face thoughtful. "That it doesn't matter. I have everything I need—everything I want—right here. I have you."

He lifted a hand to gently push aside a few wayward strands of her hair, and joy leapt through Clara like a rabbit through the spring grass.

"I have all that matters to me too," she said, letting her hands rest against his back. "But I'm glad you wrote your parents."

His eyes traced her face, and Clara thought she'd be perfectly happy, standing right here in his arms for the rest of her life. At least until he lowered his head and took her lips in a kiss, and then she decided that *this* was a much more preferable way to spend the remainder of her days. As he pressed her closer to him, she lost all track of time and place. The only thing that existed was Roman.

He pulled away slowly and with a sigh. "If I don't bring these plates out, we'll have a couple of unwanted guests knocking at the door."

Clara giggled. "By all means, we can't let Fred and Jeremiah starve." She reluctantly pulled her arms from around her husband and handed him two of the plates.

Roman balanced them in a stack, and she followed him to the door. Wrapping an arm around her and pulling her close, he dropped one quick yet head-spinning kiss to her lips. "If you don't come up to help out this afternoon, I'll hear it from the customers."

"Then I suppose I'll make the time," she said, jokingly, as if she didn't come to the stable every afternoon to assist with the customers. She opened the door for Roman and watched him walk up past the corral toward the stable. Halfway there, he turned back and smiled at her. Clara leaned against the doorframe, not even feeling the downright cold fall temperature for all the warmth she held inside.

It didn't matter what winter might bring. She'd always have summer with Roman at her side.

THANK YOU FOR READING and welcome to the Crest Stone Mail-Order Brides series! I hope you enjoyed Roman and Clara's story. If you thought this book was exciting, just wait until you read about what happens when Dora and Penny place an ad for lonely rancher Jacob Fletcher in the next book, *A Rancher's Bride*[1] (available for pre-order now).

Want to know how the little town of Crest Stone began? Find out in the Gilbert Girls series. The first book in that series is *Building Forever*[2].

Thank you SO much to all of my readers for your excitement and your patience. I'm grateful to you for every one of my books you read and for the encouragement you always provide. I owe special thank yous to the following: to Susan Shelton and Margie Harris, who both suggested the name Clara for this book's heroine; to Christina Laska, Janet Lambert, and Stacey Emanuele who named Red Hoskins, Thaddeus Jones, and Ethel Porter Hoskins; and to Elaine Barker, who suggested the name Thunder for Roman's horse.

To be alerted about my new books, sign up here: http://bit.ly/catsnewsletter I give subscribers a free download of *Forbidden Forever*, a Gilbert Girls prequel novella. You'll also get sneak peeks at upcoming books, insights into the writer life, discounts and deals, inspirations, and so much more. I'd love to have *you* join the fun!

Turn the page to see a complete list of my books.

---

1. *http://bit.ly/RanchersBride*

2.   *http://bit.ly/BuildingForeverbook*

More Books by Cat Cahill

***Crest Stone Mail-Order Brides* series**
A Hopeful Bride[1]
A Rancher's Bride[2]
***The Gilbert Girls* series**
Building Forever[3]
Running From Forever[4]
Wild Forever[5]
Hidden Forever[6]
Forever Christmas[7]
On the Edge of Forever[8]
The Gilbert Girls Book Collection – Books 1-3[9]
***Brides of Fremont County* series**

1. https://bit.ly/HopefulBride

2. http://bit.ly/RanchersBride

3. http://bit.ly/BuildingForeverbook

4. http://bit.ly/RunningForeverBook

5. http://bit.ly/WildForeverBook

6. http://bit.ly/HiddenForeverBook

7. http://bit.ly/ForeverChristmasBook

8. http://bit.ly/EdgeofForever

9. http://bit.ly/GilbertGirlsBox

Grace[10]

Molly[11]

Other Sweet Historical Western Romances by Cat

The Proxy Brides **series**

A Bride for Isaac [12]

A Bride for Andrew [13]

A Bride for Weston[14]

The Blizzard Brides **series**

A Groom for Celia [15]

The Matchmaker's Ball **series**

Waltzing with Willa[16]

---

10. http://bit.ly/ConfusedColorado

11. https://bit.ly/DejectedDenver

12. http://bit.ly/BrideforIsaac

13. https://bit.ly/BrideforAndrew

14. https://bit.ly/BrideforWeston

15. http://bit.ly/GroomforCelia

16. https://bit.ly/WaltzingwithWilla

About the Author, Cat Cahill

A SUNSET. SNOW ON THE mountains. A roaring river in the spring. A man and a woman who can't fight the love that pulls them together. The danger and uncertainty of life in the Old West. This is what inspires me to write. I hope you find an escape in my books!

I live with my family, two dogs, and a few cats in Kentucky. When I'm not writing, I'm losing myself in a good book, planning my next travel adventure, doing a puzzle, attempting to garden, or wrangling my kids.

Made in the USA
Coppell, TX
30 September 2021